REDEEMING THE DARKNESS

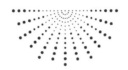

WHITNEY MORGAN

Mama Colleen
You are the reason I am who I am.
You are the reason I love romance.
I can't imagine my life without you in it.
I wish there were enough words to express my love for you, so until the english language creates the words to say, this book is for you.

I'll always remember what Matthew 19:26 means to our family.
Much love, Whit

❀ Created with Vellum

PROLOGUE

Fifteen years old

"Ivy Kendall Murphy! You better get in here right now!" Mom's voice carried from the kitchen. She'd used my full name, and that usually meant business. Dad chose the middle name when I was born, deciding to name me after Mom. She always said it was strange when she would yell it because she felt like she was yelling at herself.

"Coming!" I shouted back to her from my room. If I wasted any time responding I'd have to deal with Dad, so I hurried down. She didn't hesitate when I rounded the corner, getting right to the point of this meeting.

"Do you know who stopped me when I was leaving the school today?" she asked. I moved to the island and sat down on the bench. Mom was our school's counselor, so it didn't matter how secretly I did things, I could never hide anything from my parents. I decided playing dumb would be a mistake and opted for the truth.

"Mr. Carp?" I asked.

"Correct. Mr. Carp pulled me into his classroom and made me sit at a desk like I was a child. And do you know why he pulled me into his class?"

"Because he was missing his toupee?"

"Correct again. Ivy, that's the third time this year that his toupee has gone missing."

I tried to stifle my laugh but I couldn't. Dad walked in and seeing Mom's face; he narrowed his eyes at me.

"What happened this time, another fire?" he asked. He crossed his arms over his chest and looked even bigger than he usually did. Why did parents seem so big when you were in trouble?

"Your daughter has been stealing Mr. Carp's toupee and hiding it in other classrooms," she said. She acted as if I were doing something worse than pranking a teacher. I took my time moving my eyes toward my father. I dreaded his reaction but was surprised to see his expression.

His cheeks were twitching like he wanted to speak or smile, I wasn't sure which until I looked at his eyes and realized he was about to lose it. Laugh lines on both sides were becoming more visible as the seconds ticked by, and he eventually took a deep breath and let it out slowly.

"I'm confused," he said, tilting his head to one side like that would help him see the situation differently.

"Ivy has been stealing a hairpiece out of a teacher's classroom and hiding it around the school for him to go find, Brennan. What are you confused about?" Mom was waving her hands around like she did when she got flustered. I hated when she got flustered because I usually got grounded afterward.

"I'm sorry, babe, but I'm not prepared to handle this situation." He turned and rushed up the stairs and out of sight.

"I'm sorry," I said. I turned and looked back at my mom's disappointed face.

"I just don't understand how you keep finding it. Albert said after the teachers bring it back, he hides it in a new spot."

"His first name would be something like Albert," I fake gagged.

"Now that's just silly." She walked to the cabinet to get a glass and filled it up with water from the freezer door. "Albert is a perfectly normal name."

"Albert Carp? Nothing about that name is normal."

"Ivy, how do you keep finding his hairpiece?"

"The real question we need to ask is, why in the world does he have a toupee at school in a drawer? Do you think he's trying to impress a lady or do you think he wears it for bingo night?" I asked.

"Heaven help me! It doesn't matter why he has it. I want to know how you keep finding it."

"I look at it as a scavenger hunt," I said, shrugging my shoulders.

"But why would you want to touch it?" She let a laugh slip and tried to disguise it as a cough.

"I usually borrow the janitor's gloves."

"You steal George's gloves?" Shock covered her features.

"No, he lets me use them!" I nearly shouted, not wanting her to believe I was stealing, too. Stealing things other than Mr. Carp's toupee, that is.

"He lets you borrow them?" her eyes got a little bigger and slightly crazy looking.

"Mom, have you ever heard how Mr. Carp talks to George? It's like he's dirt or something and I can't stand it! So, me and George figured out a way to get back at the old fish."

"I can't listen to this!" She was laughing now. With no way to disguise it, she covered her ears and started walking away. "You can't scheme with other faculty members anymore, Ivy. Daniel almost lost his eyebrows last time."

"How was it my fault he lit the fire too soon? He didn't give me enough time! Mom, Daniel should have been paying attention to my signal, if you ask me!"

"Ivy! Your father and grandfather are respected, retired police officers in this town, and I work at the school. You have got to cool it with your insane pranks."

"They're not pranks," I corrected. "I'm just curious."

"Curious. And what was the goal outcome of hiding the hairpiece?" she asked.

"I don't want to say," I answered. I looked down at my hands sitting in my lap and pretended to pick something off my nails.

"Tell me," she demanded. I took a steadying breath.

"I wanted to see if he would flounder," I admitted.

My father's booming laugh broke the silence, and Mom was barely holding it in. She pointed to the stairs. "Room, now!"

"Yes, Ma'am," I said. I dragged my feet all the way up the stairs and into my bedroom. When I got to my bed, I fell face down onto my comforter.

I turned and looked at the wall to my left, staring at the pictures of cool maps I'd collected over the years.

I wanted to explore and discover things in the world. I loved all my family, but someone was always trailing me.

I wanted adventure.

I wanted to do something no one in my family had ever done before.

CHAPTER ONE

Ivy

I started talking about moving to Taylorsville, Ohio to live with my grandparents when I was sixteen years old. It hurt my mom for a long time because she thought she'd driven me away, but that wasn't the case at all. I always seemed to be the Murphy kid that broke all the rules. It didn't bother me that people saw me in that light, but when I graduated high school, I was ready to leave that brand behind.

I was ready to experience new things.

I was ready for my adventure.

Few people would think moving in with their grandparents that were in their seventies would be an adventure, but they had never met Pop and Gram.

Mom and Dad tried to convince me to stay with Grandma and Grandpa Murphy, and while I loved them and would miss them, it wasn't far enough away. I think after a while Mom finally understood moving was something I didn't just want; it was something I needed.

Pop said I could live with them and I was beyond grateful even though I wanted to work hard to get out on my own. Gram told me to take my time, but I knew I wanted to be independent more than anything. They were both so happy to have one of us living near them since we'd been a three-hour drive our entire lives.

Pop offered me a job cleaning cars and doing janitorial things at Cooper's Cars & Stuff, the business he built from the ground up, and I accepted. I became the fastest car cleaner they'd ever seen. I was technically quicker than my mother had been, and she'd worked there since she was a baby.

Three years had passed since I moved away from home, and it had been almost two years since I'd moved into a small house across the street from Cooper's. My uncle Ryan happened to be a realtor and owned a few homes in town, so I was lucky enough to rent from him. He started his business shortly after moving to Taylorsville, to be near Gram, and then stayed because he met Aunt Sam.

The day the universe decided to step in and change my life, I was working in the office in the garage. The day had gone rather smoothly, so when an angry man came in twenty minutes before closing, demanding we fix his car, I was a little thrown off.

I was number three in the chain of command. Aunt Sam ran the place. When she wasn't around, the title of 'boss' usually went to Oliver, the shop's backup manager that Pop appointed. When they were both off duty, it went to me.

In my months of being part of that chain, my worst day had been when I realized I ordered four times as much oil as our shop went through in a month. Not only was it too much, but it was also the kind we used the least. I think I sat and stared at the shipment for over an hour before I got the nerve to call Aunt Sam.

That day in June was very different, though. It happened to be my dad's birthday, and I was on the phone with him when I heard yelling near the front desk.

"Hey, dad, I've gotta hop off here. Some jerk is out there screaming at Randy, again," I said, standing to head out there.

"That poor kid gets yelled at an awful lot," he chuckled.

"Yeah, it's because he's young. These idiots don't think he knows what he's talking about, but I'll teach this one a lesson."

"Take the wrench with you," he said.

"Got it. Hope you have a good birthday, I love you."

"It would be a lot better if you were here," he said, as usual. "I love you, too, Ivy. Be careful and knock some sense into that jerk." I loved that he had complete faith in my ability to take care of things. I think it was something he learned about women when he met Mom.

After hanging up, I grabbed the large wrench off the shelf next to the door and walked out to the front desk. I came face-to-face with a man that was six feet three, at least, around two hundred pounds, and a face that conveyed enough anger to convince me he was part rodeo bull.

I was going to need a bigger wrench.

"What's the problem?" I asked, bringing the metal up and resting it on my shoulder. It landed a little too hard, and I flinched.

"Nothing for you to worry about, little girl," he snarled. I didn't believe in werewolves, but he resembled one at that moment. All that was missing was the venom dripping from his fangs.

I needed to stop watching sci-fi so late at night.

I scrunched up my nose and looked down at my frame. I was 5'4, and a half (the half was critical to me) and had enough curves to prove I was a woman. It's possible that the dark purple shirt with the pink hearts and pink shorts made me look young, but it couldn't have been that bad. My shoulder length light brown hair was a little messy because I hadn't brushed it that morning after my shower, and I may not have had a lot of makeup on, but I knew I at least had mascara framing my gray eyes. All in all, I think I looked decent enough for a twenty-one-year-old. I looked a lot better than I did when I woke up that morning!

I don't think Mom or Aunt Sam would be upset with the implication that I was the owner in this situation, so I pulled out my inner Cooper. "First of all, you twit, I'm not a little girl. I'm a stinking lady, so watch your mouth. Second of all, I run this place, so whatever your beef is with Randy, who by the way is in high school, should be with me."

He looked at Randy and me like he was waiting for the punchline of a joke.

"Did you just call me a twit?" he asked.

Had I?

I paused, going over the rant again in my head, and sure enough, I had called him a twit. I switched my weight from one foot to the other.

"I did," I admitted.

He looked from my eyes to the wrench sitting on my shoulder and pointed a large hand at it. "Why are you holding that?"

I pulled it away to look at it while I thought over my answer.

"I was probably going to hit you with it if you got out of hand," I answered.

"You were going to hit me? You would have landed me in the hospital! Do you have any idea who I am?" he practically yelled. He seemed a little angry, maybe even uptight. The man needed a coffee or a cinnamon roll or something.

"I know exactly who you are. You're the guy that needs to stop shouting before he gets knocked upside the head with a hunk of metal. I don't care if you end up in the hospital, no one is going to come in here acting like a fool and get away with it. Now, what's the problem? You might want to hurry it up with your answer before I decide your business isn't wanted here."

His hands had formed fists where they sat on the counter, and his knuckles were already white from the strain.

"I need my car fixed. I have somewhere to be in less than an hour and this is the only place that has an auto repair shop near where I'm trying to get."

"Where are you trying to get?" I asked.

"About ten miles away from here."

"And where would that be?"

"That's none of your business," he exhaled harshly. "Listen lady, can you get someone in here to fix my car or not?"

"I told him we were closing soon and that none of our guys were here to help," Randy said to me. I nodded my head and looked back at the angry man.

"What's wrong with the car?" I asked.

"My check engine light is on, and I think the back tire is low. I put air in it a couple of days ago, but something is going on with it."

"Go ahead and pull it up into this bay right here," I said, already turning and walking toward the back wall. "Randy, come watch so you can get some practice in."

I grabbed Aunt Sam's old hat and put it on to keep the hair out of my face since I didn't have a ponytail holder. I pushed my legs and arms into the coveralls and watched him pull the car in. He got out and gave me a weird look.

"You're not working on my car," he said.

"Beg your pardon, Sir, but if you want it fixed, I'll be the one to do it."

"Do you know what you're doing?"

Randy laughed, and I sent him a look that he hopefully interpreted as "shut up." It worked.

Ignoring his question, I opened his door and plugged one of our scanners into his car and waited. After a minute, the scanner told me what was wrong.

I rolled my eyes and popped the fuel door, then walked back and tightened the cap. Once I rechecked the engine light, ensuring it went off, I walked to the tire the customer said was low. I turned on my cell phone's flashlight and after searching the tire; I saw the nail.

Crap.

"You have a nail in this tire. Unfortunately, we don't keep a lot of tires here, and I know for a fact we don't have any that will work for you right now. Do you have a spare you can use for tonight? If you bring it back tomorrow, I can have a tire here by two in the afternoon." I looked up at him and he was frowning. I wasn't surprised.

"There should be a spare in the back."

I looked at him. He looked at me.

"Do you want me to change the tire?" I asked. Surely he knew how to do that.

"If you don't mind," he replied. He was looking everywhere but at me, and I hid my smile.

"Since we aren't in a bay with a car lift, we'll just do this the old-fashioned way," I said, speaking to Randy. "Go ahead and grab the tools and the jack." I looked at our customer and asked, "Where's the tire?"

He pointed to the trunk, and I opened it. Tucked underneath a piece of flooring was the spare, and I waited. After a few minutes, I peeked around the car to see the guy leaning his back against the large toolbox, and he arched his eyebrow when he made eye contact.

"I might know what I'm doing, but I can't lift this tire up out of here." He got the hint and came over to pull the tire out. He sat it beside me and I rolled it to the side where Randy was already jacking the car up.

Fifteen minutes later, and a little help with pulling one tire off and putting the other back on, we lowered the car down.

"You're all finished," I said, backing up to give him room to leave.

"How much do I owe you?" he asked. He pulled his wallet out of his back pocket and waited.

"It's on the house."

"I'm heading out, boss," Randy said from behind me. "My mom's going to be mad if I'm late for dinner again tonight."

"Just have her give me a call if she needs to, and I'll explain it was my fault," I said and waved goodbye to him.

"You have to let me pay you," he said once Randy was out of earshot.

"It's after hours. Seriously, don't worry about anything tonight. Tomorrow will be another story, though. Nothing I did tonight costs money, but tires do and my aunt will be here."

"I thought you owned this place." His eyes narrowed.

I shrugged and tried not to laugh. "I may have lied a bit. My family owns it, but I am the one in charge tonight."

"Why didn't you just say that?"

"You freaked me out with your crazy eyes and the yelling."

He pocketed his wallet and had the decency to look embarrassed. "Okay, that's fair."

Without a thank you or goodbye, my nameless customer climbed into his vehicle and drove away.

Little did I know, he'd be coming back the next day, asking for a lot more than a tire.

CHAPTER TWO

Zane

"I think this might be the stupidest thing I've ever heard come out of your mouth, Trina," I said. I was finally sitting in front of her after a hectic day, and she was spewing nonsense. I felt as if I'd wasted time driving here from a temporary stay in North Carolina. It frustrated me.

"The next time you talk to me like that, I'll whack you upside the head with my newspaper. Plus, it would only be for five years," she calmly said, as if five years was nothing.

"That is a long time!" I shouted. I took a deep breath and tried to calm down, but I couldn't. Ever since my crash and burn, I'd been trying my hardest to get on the right path, and it felt like the light at the end of the tunnel was nowhere in sight. She'd tried getting interviews on a few shows from time to time, but no one wanted anything to do with me.

They didn't trust me, and I didn't blame them. There was no way it was going to take something like this to make people believe I wasn't the same guy anymore, though.

Six years prior, at the ripe age of seventeen, I landed the role of a lifetime. As a brand new actor, they cast me in a movie they didn't think was going to be as big as it had been. It was incredible. One minute, I'm a wanna-be actor, and the next, everyone knew my name. I won't lie, the fame got to my head. I started partying, got involved with the wrong people, and ended up deep in a drug-addiction that I never saw coming. I never was the kind of person that was interested in drugs, so once I found myself in that pit, I decided staying there was what I deserved for abandoning the people that needed me.

"You don't understand, Zane. You showed up to the set of a major film so high that you caused thousands of dollars' worth of damage to the place. This is going to take time. Making sure the public, and more importantly, the producers, know you're stable will not be a walk in the park. You've got to make up for quite a bit. You put all this time and effort into being a total bust, and people lost money on you. It's time for you to put effort into showing Hollywood you're reliable again."

She had a point. As much as I wanted to get angry at her for calling me out, I couldn't. She'd stood beside me from my perfect take off all the way through to my ugly landing. She was the one that found the rehab I went to, the one that dropped me off, and the one that came back months later to pick me up.

She was the one that fought for me every time a picture would surface with rumors of more drugs, more mistakes, and more dirty laundry ready to be aired.

I remembered the moment I had my final breakdown. I was sitting at this very house with Trina and her husband, long before they had their son. I was a sloppy mess, but they didn't let me walk back out the door. They sat me down on the couch and had the smallest intervention imaginable. Just the tree of us sat and talked for hours until I finally agreed to go to rehab. They convinced me to sign my things over to Trina while I was away so she could protect everything, so I did.

She'd begged me to trust her, and I had. She never saw me as her ticket to riches; she saw a messed up kid that needed someone to step in and take control of his life. I can't imagine where I'd be if she hadn't done what was necessary.

I wouldn't even be clean if it weren't for her. I owed her everything and more.

"Alright, Trina, I'll do it."

She sighed a breath of relief and pulled out a notepad. There was a knock on the door, and before she could utter a word, a tiny version of her and her husband opened the door and ran in. Grayson, her husband, followed shortly after.

"Sorry, guys," he said. "I tried to stop him, but he was excited to see Zane."

"It's alright," I said. I picked up the wiggling two-year-old and put him on my lap. "Hey, buddy."

"Hi, Thane. Wanna play tarth with me?" he asked. He hadn't mastered all his letter sounds yet, but if you ask me, it was one of the many things that made him adorable.

"I'd really love to, but right now I have to talk to your mommy."

"Otay. Bye-bye, Thane."

"See ya later, Tan."

Tanner raced out of the room, and Grayson stayed behind. "Are you going to do it?" he asked me.

"I'm going to give it a try," I answered. Tanner had made his way back into the doorway and was tugging on his dad's pant leg.

"Good luck finding someone who will agree," he laughed. "Although a million-dollar payout makes it more appealing." He picked up Tanner and shut the door behind them as they left.

I looked at Trina, and she shot me a sad smile. "Why are you sad? I figured this would make you happy," I said.

She sighed. "Zane, I look at you like a baby brother, you know that. I care about what happens to you as a person, not as an actor. I'm willing to do whatever it takes to get you to the place you want to be career-wise, but I just get scared."

"This was your idea," I reminded her.

"I said I'm willing to help you do whatever it takes to get back in the acting game, not that I want you to do those things. My plan is solid; I know that for a fact, I just want you to be careful. You've got things you don't want to be uncovered, and having a wife can make that complicated. I just want you to understand that, I guess."

"I'm not worried about the skeletons in my closet," I said through clenched teeth. I hated when she tried to bring this up.

"I wouldn't call them skeletons when they're living, breathing beings." She cocked an eyebrow, daring me to argue, so I stood and shoved my hands into my pocket to hide the tremble. "I'll call you tomorrow and let you know her name."

She blanched. "You have someone in mind?"

"I do," I said before turning and walking out her office door.

"Good luck!" she called from behind me, and I felt a weight settle in my gut. I was going to need all the luck I could get with this one.

CHAPTER THREE

Ivy

Aunt Sam was standing outside the shop office, eyes wide, staring at something near the front. I knew what, or whom she had her gaze fixed on when I looked at the clock.

It was only a little after 1:00 PM, but my aunt's eyes told me he was early. I stood, grabbed the large wrench from the shelf, and walked out to greet him. I'd be the only one that knew who he was since Randy wasn't working. He was dressed down in jean shorts and a plain gray shirt. The shirt sleeves were pulled tight around his arms, showing off his large muscles, and I was glad I'd decided to bring my weapon.

"Again with that thing?" he asked, eyeing my shoulder.

"I don't know you, so I have to take precautions. This is my aunt, Sam," I said, pointing to the pink haired, forty-six-year-old beside me. "She's the owner."

"Technically, I'm the manager." She reached her hand out to shake his. "Can I help you with something?"

"He's the guy waiting for the tire," I supplied before he could talk. He narrowed his eyes at me after taking Sam's hand in greeting. Apparently, he didn't like people speaking for him.

"My name is Zane Landis, ma'am. I had a meeting here last night but had some car trouble. That's how I found this place."

"He didn't tighten his gas cap enough," I said, barely disguising the humor in my voice.

"And there was a nail in my tire," he added. His eyes told me he didn't like me, but they held something else I didn't think I liked. "I was wondering if I could speak to you, alone."

"Absolutely not!" the deep, angry voice from behind him said. I saw Pop when he'd walked in and hovered, listening to the conversation, but I'd decided to let him be a silent presence.

Zane turned and took in Pop like he was butting into the wrong person's business. That wasn't good. The wrench was for my safety, but at that moment I feared for Zane's.

"Can I ask you why?" Zane asked, irritation in his voice.

"Because she's my granddaughter and I'm not going to let her in a room alone with a hot head like you," he answered.

"You don't even know me," Zane replied, and for the first time in my entire life, I saw a vein in Pop's forehead grow. I'd heard about that vein.

"Oh, crap!" Aunt Sam whispered beside me. I had to take action before someone got themselves killed.

"I know exactly who you are. I might be an old man, but I

21

keep up with the times. You're that little brat from California."

"California?" I asked. I stepped forward, completely forgetting my grandfather's hard look because, well, California.

"Yeah," Zane said, looking down at me. He looked back at Pop and continued. I wasn't sure why, but his voice immediately changed. This time when he spoke, he was respectful. "If I could talk to her privately, I'd appreciate it. We could walk right there, over by the cars."

I don't know what came over me, but I tossed the wrench to Pop, hearing him grunt as he caught it before I grabbed Zane's hand and started pulling him to the car lot. Pop didn't say anything, but he didn't move, and when I stopped us near the middle of the lot, I could still see Pop leaning up against the outside of the building.

"You're from California?" I asked. Sure, I'd met people from all over, but California was one of the places I wanted to go more than I wanted my next breath.

"Do you honestly have no idea who I am?" he asked. He shook his head like he couldn't believe it.

"You're Zane. That's what you said in there. Should I know more than that?"

"I'm an actor," he said, as if he'd just told me his hair was blonde. Like it was no big thing. My eyes widened. Maybe he was lying, but if not, this was awesome. I couldn't help but feel a twinge of jealousy. It wasn't that I wanted to act because Lord knows I would make a fool of myself, but he had probably been to a lot of places. He'd probably even seen Niagara Falls.

"Have you been in any good movies?" I asked.

"Only one," he said. He ran his hand through his short-cropped hair and exhaled slowly. "I better be upfront with you before I go on. I was in a movie called Cold Hearted Ranger about five years ago." I nodded because I'd heard of the film. Never watched it, but I knew it was a huge hit, especially with my grandpa and father. Even my brothers loved it. "After the movie, I got involved in some bad things, but I got help, and I've been clean ever since. It landed me in a sticky situation with the acting world. Producers don't want me because I'm a flight risk, so, I need to appear stable. I need to look like I've settled down."

My eyes were still wide, and I was nodding like a crazy person.

"This is the craziest thing I've ever done," he said more to himself than me. "I need to ask you a question, but I want you to hear me out before you freak out, okay?"

I said nothing.

"I need a verbal confirmation you won't freak out before I explain things."

"Oh, yeah, sure," I quickly agreed.

"Okay. I need you to marry me."

Wait, what?

I froze.

Marry him?

Can't say I saw that coming.

I was almost sure he was going to ask for a free tire, which I would have done, but marriage? I don't think so.

"Wow," I started laughing. "You need new jokes, man." I turned to walk away, and he gently grabbed my arm. I turned to look into his blue eyes and waited.

"I'm not really the joking type. I'm completely serious, and I know this is asking a lot."

"You didn't even ask," I whispered.

"Huh?" he asked.

"Nothing."

"So, will you do it?"

"Is it because I'm a good mechanic? I mean, I'm sure there are lots of good ones in California. Plus, you got lucky, I don't know a lot about cars. Only the really basic stuff." It was the only thing that made sense to me.

"No, I told you I needed to look like I've settled down. Producers won't want me if it looks like I'm living in bachelorhood, partying all the time like I was when things got bad. My agent thinks if I had a wife for a while they might start looking at me differently."

"Are you sure you don't just want me to give you the tire for free? I can probably make that happen."

"I can pay for a stupid tire." He sounded frustrated.

"Don't get snippy with me, dude. You just told me to marry you, and that was weird. My brain doesn't process weird that fast, so give me a break."

"Sorry," he said. I gave myself a minute to breathe. The breathing didn't help.

"So, you need to get married? That sounds pretty insane, even for Hollywood. I don't think you being married for a few weeks is going to change people's minds."

"Five years," he said.

"Five years, what?"

"The marriage needs to be for five years. My agent has a five-year plan to get me back on the list of wanted actors. I can't do it alone, though. I need a wife."

"Because a wife is part of the plan," I sighed and started pacing. Strange things started happening in my head. It was like one of the old toys I had as a kid; you pull the lever and see a different picture. Except this was real life, and I wasn't pulling a lever or looking into a View Master. One second, I'd see some exotic place on my bucket list, then I'd see my mom's face or my dad's angry scowl.

"Exactly. A wife makes me look like I've fallen in love and chosen the family life. After a couple of years, we'll start going to parties and different functions. There's a premiere party planned in Hawaii in a few months, for example. We couldn't go to that one because of the time frame, but there will be more."

"Hawaii? Like, the place?"

"Is there another Hawaii?" he asked, confused.

"I don't think so."

"Well, then yeah, the place. I know you're from this weird hole-in-the-wall town, but you'd get to see a lot of places. I haven't even told you the best part of the deal," he said. "For the duration of the marriage, you wouldn't have to worry about anything. I'd take care of all the finances and anything you could want, you can have. Then, at the end of the five years, you'll get a payout of one million dollars."

I started hearing a weird humming noise in my ears.

"I think I should sit down," I said before climbing up onto the car behind me.

"If you're gonna pass out, why would you climb up on a car? You're gonna get hurt when you fall."

"If I pass out, I fully expect the guy who just proposed marriage to break my fall!" I almost yelled and then sighed. "I'm not going to pass out; I just need to sit."

"Are you okay?" he asked. I looked at his face. His eyes looked genuine. He didn't really seem like the type to joke about something so serious, but I'd only known him for twenty-four hours, so how would I know if I was right? I couldn't lie and say the offer didn't sound amazing. Maybe not so much the getting married part, but the getting to see the world part did. The payout sounded nice, too, but it wasn't really what made me want to say yes. The stupid, crazy adventurer wanted to say yes. I looked back at the shop where Pop was leaning against the building beside Aunt Sam. They weren't going to be okay with this.

"My family won't allow me to leave," I warned him.

"You'll have to tell them you're in love and really sell it." I almost laughed, but the desperation in his eyes took the desire to do so away.

"I don't want to lie. I've always been honest with my family."

"It's part of the deal. I really need this to work, so if you don't think you can do it, I'll need to find someone else."

"I guess it wouldn't be hard for them to believe. My mom always tells me I'm the nutty kid."

"Is that a yes?" he asked.

"Can I have some time to think about it?" I asked.

"I wish I could say yes, but we would have to leave quickly."

"California?"

"I live in Denver full time, but we'd need to leave to get married."

"Hm." That didn't seem like the right response, but I was having trouble putting a lot of words together.

"I know this is crazy, but I need an answer pretty quickly."

"I want to say yes, but my family will try to kill you before they let you drive off with me."

"Then don't tell them," he begged.

"I don't want to lie, even if it is by omission. Plus, don't we need a marriage license or something?"

"Marriage is simple in Las Vegas," he answered.

"I've always wanted to see Las Vegas," I said to myself. I felt my breathing start to speed up, but I felt happiness, too. How old do you have to be before you know your intuition is right? Saying yes felt right. I couldn't explain it, and if I over thought it, I would just doubt myself.

"Listen, give me your number, and when I head out tomorrow, I'll come pick you up. Don't tell anyone until we get far enough away so no one tries to kill me."

"You underestimate my family," I took a deep breath. "This is crazy. I don't know you enough to run away and marry you."

"Look at it for what it is; it's a huge adventure."

I looked into his eyes and searched for a feeling, absolutely anything telling me this would be a mistake. A nagging feeling that would tell me not to go and to stay in Taylorsville.

"Tomorrow I'll come get you, and you can read the contract on the way to the airport."

"I have to sign a contract?" I asked.

"It only states that you can't try to take more money from me at the end. It's broken down really well, and if you don't agree with something, I can bring you back."

This was stupid. I was fighting a losing battle against my smile. I felt like this was the moment I'd been waiting for all my life.

"I'll do it," I said confidently. "I'll marry you."

"You will?" His shock surprised me. He acted as if he'd not just spent the last ten minutes trying to convince me to marry him.

"Isn't that the response you wanted?" I asked.

"Of course. I just didn't think you'd actually say yes."

"Why did you ask me?"

He hesitated. "Honestly, because you have absolutely no idea who I am."

"Oh." It wasn't as if I wanted him to claim I was pretty, but I mean, a compliment would have been nice since I was about to pledge five years to the guy. I guess I couldn't blame him, though. I wasn't exactly tooting his horn, either.

He pulled out his phone and handed it to me, but I almost dropped it because my hands were shaking. After putting my number in, I handed it back.

"By the way, my name is Ivy Murphy," I said, reaching out my hand. He looked at it a second before taking my hand in his.

"Zane." He gave me a polite smile that didn't quite reach his eyes.

"Nice to meet you, Zane. I guess I'll see you in the morning."

He took a step back and then stopped. "You have to convince your family that you love me. I'm not too keen on dying this young."

"How old are you?" I asked before he could leave.

"Twenty-three. You? Please tell me you're over eighteen." He looked like he might throw up and I laughed.

"Twenty-one. You're in the clear." I smiled. "Don't worry about me; I'll convince them. We should wait to tell them after we get married, but I'll do my part as long as you promise me adventure."

"I promise," he said, then he turned and started walking back to the shop.

"Wait!" I called out. He stopped and turned to look at me. "Text me, so I have your number, in case I change my mind."

He didn't respond, but I guess I didn't really expect him to.

They must have replaced the tire while we were talking because he pulled out after only a few minutes. With a final wave goodbye, he drove past where I was still sitting on one of the cars and away he went.

He never did text me.

CHAPTER FOUR

Ivy

When I got home from work, the excitement had slightly worn off, and some fear settled in the pit of my stomach. I didn't have any idea who this man was, and I'd just agreed to marry him. Of course, I could take it back and not leave with him when he showed up, but I honestly didn't want that.

I made my way to the living room and sat down on the recliner. My stomach rumbled, and I wondered what I had in my fridge. I hadn't gone to the grocery store in two weeks, but I guess if I was leaving, I didn't need groceries.

"What in the world is happening to my life?" I asked out loud.

"I have no idea," a voice answered. I started screaming. Like, my throat was going to bleed because I was screaming so loud.

"Ivy!" the voice yelled again, and I opened my eyes to see my cousin Callahan come out of the spare bedroom. He laughed so hard he had to lean against the wall for support. I wanted to kill him.

"What are you doing?" I yelled. I took a calming breath in through my nose and shot daggers with my eyes. "You scared the crap out of me!"

He was still laughing. "Oh, man, that was brilliant!"

"How did you get in my house?" I asked.

"I asked Ryan to let me in earlier," he grinned.

"Why?"

"I came to town to spend the weekend with you." He took a seat on the couch and got comfortable.

"Where's your car?"

"I parked it in the store parking lot so you wouldn't see it."

Well, this was going to be a problem.

"Cal," I said. He must have heard something in my voice because his eyes shot to mine and he sat up.

"What's going on?" he asked.

"I have to swear you to secrecy."

"On my life, you already know that."

Cal was my best friend. He was my only friend, and it didn't matter that he was my cousin, we were just best friends. Too similar in too many ways.

"I met someone yesterday," I started. I told him about Zane coming in to get work done on his car and how he came back, asking me if I'd marry him. I told him who he was and why he wanted me to marry him. I told Cal everything.

"What's his name?"

"Zane Landis," I answered.

His eyes went wide. "No way! Ivy, he's that guy in that ranger movie!"

"That's what he said."

Cal took his phone out and started typing away. He showed me the screen, and I saw a slightly younger version of Zane staring back at me.

"Is this him?" he asked. I nodded. "Wow, you're going to be famous."

"You're assuming I said yes."

"I know you said yes. You'd be an idiot if you said no and you're no idiot. Plus, you wouldn't look conflicted if you'd already said no."

"You think I should do it?" I asked.

He placed his phone down and moved to the coffee table, so he was sitting directly in front of me. He rested his elbows on his knees and smiled at me.

"I think you're one of the strongest people I know. You're smart, and you have a lot of energy. If there's anyone that could do this and make it work, it's you. I think you should take advantage of an opportunity that's staring you in the face. Tell me what I need to do, and I'll help you."

A memory of something crazy we'd done when we were children struck me, not that we were much more mature as adults. "Do you remember when we were kids and our dads took us camping?"

"The one and only time they did? Yeah," he chuckled. "I remember."

"Poor guys. Mom told them not to do something like that, but they didn't believe the trouble we'd get into."

"You're the one that got stuck in the tree; I was only trying to help you get down."

I narrowed my eyes. "That is not true, and you know it. If you hadn't wanted to race, I would have never climbed that high in the first place."

"What kid doesn't dream of racing someone up a tree? It was like, ingrained in my soul or something."

"We raced up the tree and, instead of calling out when you got scared so I'd stop climbing, you let me climb so high that my dad had to call the fire department to come get me down."

Cal fell backward on the table, laughing so hard he grabbed his stomach. I couldn't hold it in, and I joined him. The look on Dad's face when the firefighters got me down was priceless.

"Shortest camping trip in the history of the world, I think," I giggled.

"I think our dads were so shocked that they didn't know whether to be mad or proud."

"Well, mine grounded me when I got home," I admitted.

"Mine too," he shook his head and smiled. "So, what's it going to be, Ivy? Are you going to take a risk? See how high you can climb in the adventure of life?"

I grinned.

"I need to pack some bags."

"That's the Ivy I know and love!"

"And I need you to act like you have no idea what's going on, Cal, no matter who you're around. Even if it's just you and I talking, you can't say a word, just in case there's a chance of someone listening. I can't let Zane know I told you, at least not yet, because I don't want him to get upset."

"Well, it sounds like I came for a surprise visit just in time," he laughed. "Let's go pack some bags."

We stood and made our way to my room. Callahan

helped me until the early morning hours, and then, after a hug goodbye, he left.

CHAPTER FIVE

Ivy

I found a piece of notebook paper and wrote a goodbye note to my family. Pop had a key to my house along with Uncle Ryan, so I knew when I didn't show up for work the next day, they'd find it. This was definitely the worst thing I'd ever done. Probably the worst thing I would ever do in my life. I hoped it was, at least.

Rereading the note made me cringe. Even I didn't believe it.

Dear Pop, Uncle Ryan, Aunt Sam, Mom, Dad and anyone else that is reading this.

First, I want to apologize for leaving like this, but I'm getting married! I know you are probably beyond worried, but you have nothing to worry about. I've fallen in love! It's true! I promise to call you all when we get situated and let you know everything.

I promise you; I am fine. Please don't hate me, please don't be too upset with me. I know what I'm doing, and I promise everything will be okay. I'll see you soon.

Love you all,

Ivy

IT WAS STILL DARK OUT, but Zane had called me at two in the morning, right after Cal left, to let me know he was going to pick me up at three.

Thankfully, just a few weeks prior I had ordered my very first luggage set for my future travels, so I had something in which to pack my stuff.

Two rolling suitcases, a duffle bag, two small zipper bags, my purse and a backpack were sitting by the door holding all my belongings. All the belongings I could take with me, anyway.

I quickly made a pot of coffee and filled two travel mugs. With no idea how Zane took his coffee, I grabbed two extra vanilla creamer packets and shoved them in my purse. I did a quick run through of my house, checking to make sure I had forgotten nothing important, and before I knew it, there was a knock at the front door.

Zane didn't look like a morning person.

"Ready?" he asked. His voice was husky, like he wasn't quite awake yet.

"Yeah, I have to get all of my bags though."

"Why are you taking bags?" He sounded irritated. I fought the urge to roll my eyes and almost lost.

"Why wouldn't I take my things? I'm supposedly moving away for five years. I don't want my family to have to come and pack up all my things. Plus, they're my things."

"I just thought you'd buy new stuff. You're going to be rich."

"Not for another few years, I won't."

"You're going to be my wife; therefore, you're going to be rich."

"I don't care. I want my stuff," I said. I picked the coffee mugs up off the table and headed out to the car. I opened the door and placed them in the cup holders, then turned to walk back inside.

"You can help me with these," I said. Zane was staring at my suitcases like he wished they would burst into flames. Thankfully, he grabbed everything except one bag on rollers and took them to the car, piling them in the backseat.

I turned and looked through the door, into the house that had been my home and felt a twinge of sadness. I reminded myself that I was doing something I would never get another opportunity to do, so I couldn't pass this up. I didn't think anyone ever got a chance like this.

"Come on," Zane said from directly behind me. He took the suitcase out of my hand, and I shut and locked my door.

"I brought you coffee," I said when we climbed into the car. "I wasn't sure if you took sugar or cream, but I have some vanilla creamer if you want it."

"That would be great. Do you mind putting it in for me?" We'd been on the road for almost five minutes, and we were already almost out of Taylorsville.

The only times I'd ever been outside of Ohio were the few vacations our family went on. I'd never been out as far as we were going, though.

"So how are we getting to Las Vegas?"

"I bought plane tickets last night. We're meeting my agent at the airport so she can watch you sign the contract, and then she's going to hire someone to drive the car to my house in Denver. You can't take all your bags on the plane. Only the small one."

The "small one" he was referring to was my purse. I had no idea what I even had inside.

"I think I have a knife in here," I admitted, picking it up to look through it.

"Are you kidding me? Why are you carrying a weapon?"

Sure enough, I pulled out my pocketknife and held it up to show him. He flinched like he thought I'd cut him and I scoffed.

"I carry a knife around because my gun won't fit in this thing." I joked.

"You have a gun?" He looked like he didn't believe me.

"I do. I don't have it here, though. It's back at home with my parents."

"What am I doing?" he whispered.

"So, where's the contract?" I asked. I got out the creamer and poured it into his coffee, then handed it to him. He thanked me and pointed to the glove-box.

I opened it and pulled out a legal-looking envelope with the words, "Mr. Zane Landis" on it and in small print below, it read, "Mrs. Ivy Landis".

Reading that felt as normal as a swift kick to the kidney.

"Before I read this, I want to add one stipulation of my own," I said, staring at the envelope.

"What's that?"

"I don't know you. I'm literally going with my gut feeling about you, and that's as stupid as walking into oncoming traffic, but I feel good about this. I just want you to understand one thing about me, though," I turned my body in my seat so I could look at him. "I don't care who you are, and I don't care about serving time in prison. As God as my witness, if you ever lay a harmful finger on me, I will cut you."

"Those are some mighty big words coming from someone so tiny," he said, taking a quick look at me.

"I'm not lying. On my life, I promise, I will make you regret it."

"Calm down. I'd never hurt you or any other woman, but let me explain something, too. This marriage may be a farce, but I expect you to treat it like a real one. There will be no dating other people while we're married. I don't share my things."

"Your things?" I asked, feeling my nose scrunch up. Gross.

"I'm not going to share my wife. I expect you to be faithful to me during this period. I don't want the media catching you with another man and making it look like I can't even keep my wife."

"You could always say please," I suggested. He didn't reply. "I will promise you my faithfulness if you ask me nicely."

"How did I find the most complicated woman on earth?" he asked. He took a deep breath and his facial expression reminded me of what Duke looked like when Mom made him eat veggies. "Will you please refrain from dating other guys while we're married?"

"Of course," I said automatically, then I tore into the envelope. Zane mumbled something incoherent, and I felt my lips twitch.

I don't know what I was expecting, but the contract was a

mere piece of blank paper with a list of demands I had to agree to, with a line at the very bottom for Zane and me to sign. It was weird.

Both parties entering into this agreement have entered on their own accord.
They will decide any personal relationship between parties.
Neither party is permitted to talk about the agreement with anyone other than those listed in this agreement.
Ivy will be paid a total of One Million dollars at the end of this five-year arrangement.

I TUCKED the contract back into the glove compartment and rolled down the window, so I could breathe. It was more than real at that point. I was deciding to become someone's wife at twenty-one years old. That seemed incredibly young to me. I mean, maybe it wasn't too young, but I still wore hearts and stars on my clothes for Pete's sake. My biggest goal in life was to travel, and now I was doing the one thing that could either help me reach that goal or take it all away.

Marriage.

What in the world?

"Everything okay?" Zane asked after giving me a few minutes to soak up what I'd read. It wasn't anything new but reading it on paper was a bit odd. I couldn't help but feel guilty for telling Cal, but I reminded myself I hadn't signed anything at that point.

"Everything is good. I just can't believe I'm doing this."

* * *

"THERE'S MY AGENT," Zane said a couple of hours later when we pulled into the airport. I looked up to see a beautiful woman with long blonde hair waiting beside a minivan. I wasn't expecting the van. We both got out and walked over to her.

"Hello, you must be Ivy." Her smile was friendly, but her eyes looked worried. "I'm Trina, Zane's agent. I assume you've looked over the agreement?"

"I did, but I forgot it in the car." I turned and jogged back to Zane's vehicle and pulled the envelope out. "Here you go," I said handing it to her when I returned.

She pulled a stamp out of her bag and then placed the contract on the van so I could sign.

Without any hesitation, Zane grabbed the pen and signed his name. I tried to be as confident as he was, reminding myself that Zane was the one losing something in this deal. One million dollars wasn't a small fee. I picked up the pen and signed my name as clearly as I could. I wished my name had been a bit longer because before I knew it, his agent notarized my signature and she was driving away.

"Come on; we've got to get a move on." Zane took my hand and pulled me behind him. We zigzagged through the herds of people in the airport, and I was told to wait while he did something at the counter.

It was nearly an hour and a half later before we were walking through the gate to board our plane. We found our seats, and I was thankful that they were able to seat us together with it being last minute.

They sandwiched me between Zane and another man I guessed to be around thirty-five or forty. I stared straight ahead, though, because something I'd failed to mention to Zane was that I'd never been on a plane, and I had a genuine fear of falling to my death.

"You have to put your seatbelt on," I heard the stranger beside me whisper. I looked over and returned his friendly smile.

"Thank you," I laughed. "I've never been on a plane before, so I'm kind of nervous."

"I can tell. Your hands are shaking," he said, pointing to my hands. "I'm Oliver, but my friends call me Ollie. Since you and I are going to be seat companions for a few hours, you might as well call me Ollie, too."

"Hello Ollie, I'm Ivy." I lifted my hand from my lap to reach over and shake his, but before I got very far, I felt a large hand wrap around my wrist and pull it into another lap. I looked down and saw Zane's hands holding mine.

It seemed loving, but when I looked into his dark blue eyes, I saw a warning and felt my blood boil.

This was going to be a long flight.

CHAPTER SIX

Zane

I pulled Ivy's hand into my lap as soon as I saw her make a move to touch the guy beside her. It had only been a few hours since I discussed my terms and she was already going back on her word. My eyes narrowed in warning to her and her own blazed back at me.

She looked back at Oliver and shook his hand with her other one. I fought the urge to growl in irritation.

"Sorry about him. He's just super into me right now since we're getting married." She patted my hand, and the loser beside her laughed.

There were very few people I trusted. Trina and her husband, and the woman I hired to be my cook. I didn't even trust the cleaning lady, who happened to be the cook's granddaughter. For some unknown reason, I trusted Ivy enough to ask her to marry me and keep the real reason for our marriage a secret.

"Where's your ring?" I heard the guy ask, and it grated on my nerves. I didn't like nosey people. I opened my mouth to speak, but Ivy beat me.

"Well, you see, we've actually just decided to get married. It was kind of a whirlwind thing. I was slaving away at my family's business, daydreaming about running away, and then my knight in shining armor came in and whisked me away."

She was laying it on thick and making it sound awful. I knew she was irritated with me, I not only heard it in her voice but she kept trying to pull her hand out of my grasp. Fat chance.

"Isn't that right, babe?" she asked, and I looked down at her. She had her hair pulled up into something that looked like a rat's nest on top of her head, and she had a coffee spot on her bright yellow t-shirt, directly above the word, 'Love' spelled in pink letters.

It seemed she was a girl trapped in a woman's body. Despite that fact, she was beautiful. When she asked why I chose her, I'd been honest in saying it was because she had no idea who I was, but I intentionally left out the part about her looks.

The minute Trina told me about her plan, I thought of the pretty, wrench-wielding girl I'd met earlier that day. I had no intention of falling in love and making any kind of connection, but I was human. I could admit I wanted to be at least a little attracted to the woman I was going to be marrying.

I knew better than to think I was healthy enough to want someone forever.

Without answering, I let my head fall back onto headrest and closed my eyes. I could still feel her gaze, and when she stopped trying to tug her hand out of my grasp, I relaxed.

"Are you sure you want to marry him?" I heard Oliver whisper. I sighed.

"Yeah, I want to marry him. Sometimes he's uncomfortable being around a lot of people," she said.

She didn't know how right she was. Ever since my downward spiral in the public eye, anyone and everyone became my enemy. Tabloids that had been my biggest supporters and fans quickly became the voice that fueled hatred. Article after article ran my name through the mud, and even after rehab, they were still at it. It wasn't until about a year ago that they seemed to forget I existed.

At first, I didn't know which was better; to be the Hollywood pariah or to let everyone forget who I am, but I was grateful my life had grown quiet.

"So, where are you guys headed?" Oliver asked. What kind of stupid question was that? Did average people just pry into other people's business so carelessly?

"Vegas!" she answered, excitedly. I opened my eyes and looked over at Oliver.

"Listen, buddy; I don't like the fact you're asking such personal questions, so why don't you go ahead and leave my girl alone, yeah?" His eyes widened a bit, and he nodded his head in response.

Expecting daggers, it surprised me to see a contemplative look on Ivy's face.

"Why are you looking at me like that?" I asked.

"I was just thinking that I left my family and all I have is you now. If you scare every single person away from being my friend, I'm going to grow to hate you." She was whispering so only I could hear, but Curious Joe was trying to catch her words.

I leaned in close, so my lips touched her ear, and she stiffened in response.

"I'm extremely private about every detail of my life, Ivy. That includes you, now, and to be honest with you; I don't care if you hate me. I'm not marrying you, so you'll be my friend." I pulled away and settled back into my chair. She tried to tug her arm away, but I tightened my grip, and she let out an annoyed huff.

Why couldn't this have been a boat so the Captain could marry us? I should have been more careful about how I spoke to her for those few hours because, for all I knew, she'd run off and leave me back at square one.

She signed the contract. I reminded myself.

I wasn't sure how much time went by, but the Pilot came over the intercom and introduced himself. Moments later we were being lifted into the air, and I felt Ivy's hand squeeze mine.

Apparently, that wasn't enough for her because she grabbed my bicep with her other hand and put her head on my shoulder. I heard her talking under her breath and leaned down so I could listen to her better.

She was praying. I couldn't help but smile. She was scared to death, and it was funny. This was the woman that wanted to knock me over the head with a giant tool, after all.

I intertwined our fingers to try to comfort her.

CHAPTER SEVEN

Ivy

Four hours.

For four hours, I fought an insane anxiety attack while I was thousands of feet in the air. I was sure I'd lost blood flow in my fingers on the hand Zane was holding, and I couldn't tell you for sure, but I was confident I'd drawn blood from his arm.

Finally, the plane landed, and I felt like I might throw up from pure relief. I let go of Zane's arm, and he released my hand for the first time in almost five hours. I tried to relax until we were ready to exit.

My legs were shaking so badly that I thought I was going to fall at any moment. I let out a whimper when we got into the central part of the airport, and I saw how far I was going to need to go.

"What's wrong?" Zane asked me over the chaos.

"My legs feel like jello. I think my nerves from the plane are finally catching up with me."

"No, I'd say your nerves did just fine on the plane. I'll probably have scars from your fingernails on my arm forever."

"I'm sorry," I felt tears pool in my eyes. "I'm not a cryba-by," I said to him. "I'm just getting overwhelmed right now."

"Is it the marriage?" he asked. He sounded so scared I might say yes, and as much as it should have been a contributing factor, it wasn't.

"No, it's my legs. They feel weird, and I'm drained and hungry. All that together is just too much for me to deal with at the same time."

He looked like he might laugh, but thankfully he didn't.

"Hop up on that chair," he said, pointing to an empty seat near us. "Stand up on it."

I did what he said and waited for more instructions as he stood in front of me with his back to me.

"Climb on."

I didn't even hesitate. I pushed my purse higher on my arm and grabbed onto my fiancé. He grabbed my legs and hoisted me up a little more, then started walking through the crowd. I leaned my head on my arm, so my mouth was close to his ear and whispered, "Thank you."

He didn't respond. I'd already noticed he had a habit of doing that.

When we got outside, he walked up to a cab and opened the door. He let me down before we climbed inside.

"We're going to the strip," he told the driver, and we pulled away from the curb.

The driver dropped us off in front of a casino that had dancing women dressed as flamingos out front. Zane climbed out, and I followed him up onto the sidewalk after he paid the driver.

"Listen," he said, tucking a finger under my chin, drawing my wide eyes away from all the activity going on around us. "Don't make eye contact and whatever you do, don't take anything from anybody. I don't care if they tell you it's a business card, you don't touch anything."

"Will someone try to kill me or something?" I asked. He was freaking me out.

"What? No! Everyone is trying to sell something out here. I don't have time to get stopped thirty times before we get to a church."

Oh.

"Okay, well, let's go then."

He started walking, and I had to jog to keep up. He was in a serious hurry.

We quickly made our way down the strip, and everything seemed to catch my eye. I didn't think this place would be so alive this early in the morning since all the movies showed the nightlife, but there were people everywhere. Some you could tell had been out all night, but others were wide awake and vibrant, ready for a brand new day.

Every single building we passed held something new to catch my eye. Giant signs that had more lightbulbs than the whole town of Taylorsville were lit up all over the place. Advertising casinos, restaurants, and buildings that I couldn't tell the nature of the business. There were things I saw that made me laugh and other things that made me blush. After ten minutes of walking, I was beginning to understand why Zane called Taylorsville a hole-in-the-wall town.

* * *

Just like that, we were standing in front of an impersonator. Just like every single cliche Vegas wedding I'd ever witnessed in the movies, I was being married by a guy in a white jumpsuit and glasses, with diamonds on the sides. His wig was a little off center, but I can't say that bothered me as much as the giant pimple that sat at the tip of his nose.

I looked at the pews where the couple we'd met in the lobby sat. Zane asked them to be our witnesses, and they agreed. Their ceremony didn't seem to last that long at all. Not as long as ours was lasting. It felt like he was adding in words because I could have sworn I'd been standing up there for an hour.

"Now you go ahead and lay one on her, Son." The man said. He did a little hip wiggle, and I wanted to laugh.

"That's okay," I said. "We're not ones for public displays of affection. We'd rather just kiss in-," Zane grabbed my face and brought his lips down onto mine, cutting off any further words from my mouth.

"Oh dear," I mumbled, my eyes as big as saucers. I probably should have mentioned I'd never actually kissed anyone. I mean, unless I counted my two-second lip lock with Ryker Finch. I didn't count it though because he was brand new to town and I didn't even know his name when it happened. I especially didn't tell anyone since a few months later my sister started dating his younger brother.

He pulled away and stared into my eyes. "Did you say something while I kissed you?"

"Yes."

"Want to repeat it?"

"No."

"Are you going to be a thorn in my side our whole marriage?" he asked. I thought about it for a minute, but it was hard to concentrate since he still had his hands on my cheeks.

"You know there was a man in the Bible that was thankful for the thorn in his flesh?"

"I don't think his thorn's name was Ivy."

"Technically, it really could have been. It never said what it was."

"Right. Well, let's go. We need to get home, and we've got," Zane looked at his phone, and I glanced down. It was seven in the morning where we were. "Two hours to get back to the airport to catch the flight."

"You mean we aren't staying?" I asked. My shoulders sagged with my disappointment.

"No. We're not staying." He turned and walked down the aisle toward the door. Once there, he looked over his shoulder and said, "Come on, Ivy."

I quickly waved goodbye to all the strangers that had been a part of my wedding and followed Zane. He hailed another cab, and we were again on our way to get back on a plane.

It sucked. I wanted to explore, but all I'd gotten to do was get married.

I was barely paying attention to anything the entire time we were going through security, and I was sitting on the plane before I knew it.

On the way to Denver, Zane and I were alone in our row. I didn't pay attention to the plane taking off, and I didn't reach out to him for comfort. I was scared to death, but I'd been excited to see a new place, and he ultimately ruined it.

"Let me know when you're done pouting. There are some things we need to talk about," Zane said a few hours later when we got into yet another cab.

"I'm not pouting."

"Yes, you are because you didn't get to walk around and throw money down the drain."

"Oh, big deal. So I wanted to lose a little money, sue me why don't you? I've never been there. I wanted to see it."

My cell phone interrupted us. I looked at the caller ID and saw my mom's face.

Crap.

My heart started pounding furiously in my chest, and I tried doing the math in my head. If Denver was two hours behind Ohio's time, that meant it was two in the afternoon, and my family had most definitely found my letter.

"Oh, no!" My eyes shot to Zane's. "It's my mom."

"Answer it. You can tell them you got married. There's not a lot they can do about it now." I nodded and answered the phone.

"Hello?"

"Ivy? Thank God! Where are you? Are you okay? Ryan called, and we've been calling you for over an hour!"

"I'm fine; I left it in the note. I, uh, I got married." I felt bile rise.

"You what?" My dad's voice was so loud I had to pull the phone away from my ear. Zane must have heard because he looked over and cocked an eyebrow.

"Hi daddy," I said, barely above a whisper. I felt a lump form in my throat.

"I hope you're lying," he said.

"I'm not lying. We flew to Vegas early this morning, and we got married."

"Who did you marry?"

"Uh, Zane Landis?"

"Are you asking me or telling me?" he demanded.

"Telling. I married Zane."

"Who the heck is Zane Landis?" I was going to answer, but I heard my mom's quiet voice in the background. "This has got to be the stupidest prank you've ever pulled. It's not funny! Where are you, Ivy?"

"I'm in Denver."

Everyone was silent for a moment, and I looked up to see our driver looking between the road and the mirror.

"Ivy?" My mom's voice came back over the line.

"Hi, Mom."

"I can't believe you left a note, thinking that would make us all feel better about what you did."

"I was scared to tell Pop and Gram! I didn't want anyone to stop me."

"Of all the things you've ever done, I think this takes the cake. I mean, you want to think you're an adult because you're in your twenties, but this kind of thing makes you seem more immature."

I didn't know how to reply to that.

"I have no idea how to express my disappointment in you. One day, you're going to have a daughter and then you'll understand what you've done is selfish. My father called here hysterical, Ivy. He was crying."

"Oh, Mom, I'm so, so sorry. Please believe me." If there was one thing I knew about my mother, it was that she and her father had a bond no one could ever replicate. Pop had been her mom and dad her whole life. There were no words to explain what she'd go through if anything ever happened to him.

"Do you know when I saw Pop cry last?" she asked.

"I don't know."

"Never, Ivy Kendall. I have never seen or even heard my

father cry. Never! So, how do you think it makes me feel that my daughter that he loves so much, that gave him hope of one of his grandkids running the business, just disappears without a word?"

"I don't know what else to say, Mom. I can't change what I did."

"Would you, if you could? Would you go back and change it?"

"Honestly, I don't think so. I hate that, but I won't lie to you." She let out a sigh that sounded as if the entire world came to rest on her shoulders.

"Ivy, what have you done? Are you pregnant? Is that what's going on?"

"No, I'm not pregnant. I'm just in love," I said without much conviction. "Dad?" I asked.

"He's not here anymore. He went outside to tell your brothers and sisters. Honey, I know you think what you did was alright, but if you got married, you took something really special away from your father."

"How? I figured I couldn't tell you guys because you'd try to stop me."

"Of course we would have tried to stop you. We don't even know this boy other than what's been on the news. You took away your dad's first opportunity to give away one of his daughters. He didn't get to walk you down the aisle."

The lump grew until I had tears falling down both cheeks. "I didn't think about that."

"I know you didn't."

"I'm sorry, Mom."

"I'm just so confused. I only spoke to you two days ago. Why didn't you tell me about Zane?"

"It was all kind of fast, to be honest. It wasn't something I had planned."

"I just want you to come home. I want to know you're safe." I heard her sniffle and knew she was crying, too.

"I'm safe." I looked at my husband and wondered if I was being truthful, but I knew in my gut that I was. "I promise I'm safe."

"Your dad is going to need some time. I don't know if he's ever been more hurt by something. There's something else I wanted to tell you, though. Your Uncle Jackson called this morning. He said Callahan got hurt this morning. He was out playing lacrosse with some of his friends, and I guess he took a stick to the kneecap."

"What? When? Is he going to be okay?" I'd only seen Cal yesterday. Had I not left, he would probably be safe at my house today.

"Jackson seems to think he's okay, but it happened early this morning. He's really upset though. He had that mountain climb scheduled for next month, and there's no way he can do that now. I think he would like to hear from you."

"I'll give him a call. I can't believe he can't go next month. He was so excited."

"I know, but I think he has the willpower to work hard on healing."

"He does," I agreed.

"I don't want to hang up," she said. "But I need to go check on your dad."

"Mom?"

"Yeah?"

"Do you hate me?" I asked, quietly.

"Sweetheart, I could never, ever hate you. I love you so much, and it's because I love you that I feel hurt. I wish you'd told me that you were in love and wanted to get married. I wish I'd known about the person you now call your husband."

"I was just scared to say something about it. I'm sorry."

"So, you thought leaving a job without notice and abandoning a house was better?" she asked.

Guilt came crashing down on me, and I hesitated. "It makes this so much worse, but I didn't think about those things. I can get another job and pay rent until Ryan finds someone to live in the house, and I figured the shop wouldn't miss me. I'm an idiot, I know."

"I shouldn't even say this, but I think everyone already forgave you."

I sighed. "I really am sorry, Mom. I wish I could rewind and change how I left."

"Unfortunately, you can't do that. Just, please, be careful. I love you, Ivy. Promise me you'll come home. Promise you will call me if you need anything at all."

"I promise, and I love you too."

We disconnected, and I took a few deep breaths. I was grateful when Zane acted as if the conversation that just took place didn't happen because I don't know if I could have handled talking about my family.

A few minutes went by before I finally asked what he wanted to talk to me about before my mom called.

"When we get to the house, you're going to meet my cook, Rayna, and my maid, Zariah. They've worked for me for a few years now, but I don't trust the maid. Be careful what you say around them. You're also going to meet your bodyguard."

"Wait, what? Why on earth do I need a bodyguard?" I almost yelled.

"Are you joking? You need to protection at all times. You're not going to be able to just go to the store whenever you want. I've never met him, but Trina said she found someone willing to do it and he's supposed to meet us at the house."

"So, he'll know?"

"No, he knows that we need a bodyguard for five years. No one outside of you, me, and Trina know."

Cal knows, I thought.

"But I didn't think people even paid attention to you anymore. Plus, it's Denver, not Los Angeles."

"It doesn't matter. You have to have protection. He'll be staying in the apartment above the garage, so he's always going to be around. Consider this your warning that you'll have a shadow for the next five years."

It stunned me into silence. It couldn't get any worse than having your own personal babysitter at twenty-one.

CHAPTER EIGHT

Ivy

We pulled into the driveway of a pretty average looking house. It was big, by my standards, but it seemed ordinary, other than the giant window. I don't know what I'd been expecting. A castle maybe? I mean, he was a millionaire.

Instead of a large, gated-in home, it was a simple two-story house. The apartment my bodyguard would stay in was above the garage.

Just thinking about the bodyguard left a nasty taste in my mouth. Who does that kind of thing? Why hire a bodyguard for your wife?

The more I thought about it, the more normal hiring someone seemed for an actor or actress. And, even if I'd never seen his movie, Zane Landis was an actor.

He opened the door, and we walked into a long hallway. To the right was the entryway to the kitchen, and to the left was the living room. I had a feeling I wasn't going to like that room because the entire front wall was made up of a large window. No blinds, no curtains, just a window. Not even a window you could open, so I guess it could be considered a glass wall. It was creepy, so I definitely wouldn't be spending time downstairs in the middle of the night.

Zane quickly walked around the house, briefly uttering what each room was. There was a basement that housed a theater room, a small gym, and his personal office. The master bedroom, a spare bedroom, and a couple restrooms were all on the second floor. I figured the spare would belong to me, but I was quickly proven wrong.

He led us into the master bedroom, and I waited by the door.

"Which room is mine?" I asked. He looked around like the question confused him.

"What do you mean? This is your bedroom, too."

Wait, what?

"I'm sorry, I don't understand. Where are you sleeping?"

"I'm sleeping in the bed next to my wife."

"I'm really confused."

"Look, I have a staff of people working here. I can't have my wife sleeping in another room. You're safe; I promise you that you're safe. I just need you tp sleep in here. Please don't make this difficult."

"I'm not trying to be difficult; I'm just a little stunned. You didn't mention it before."

"Well," he lifted his arms up and let them drop. "Surprise."

I let out an awkward laugh. "This is going to make for a fascinating few years. I don't like this."

"Why are you so determined to give me an ulcer?"

"Are you kidding me? I'm the one that just moved away

from home and married a man I don't even know. How on earth are you the one getting the ulcer?"

"I thought you'd be a lot more docile."

"How flattering. No wonder you had to con someone into being your wife."

"I didn't con you!"

"Well, you certainly weren't very forthcoming about all the circumstances." He stared at me like he didn't know what I was saying. "I need a bodyguard, and I have to sleep in here! It should be obvious why I'm upset."

"Would that have made you say no?" he asked.

"Yes! No. I don't know! This is just all so weird. I thought I'd have a separate room."

"I'm sorry to disappoint."

"Maybe we could just get rid of the staff?"

"You want to fire someone who has been working for me for years? If so, you can take care of it."

"That certainly isn't going to happen."

"I don't understand what the big deal is here. People go through arranged marriages all the time. Why can't you just look at it like that?"

"That's all fine and dandy, but you're not getting my point here. I don't know you. Marrying you was basically the epitome of stupid things to do with a stranger. Sleeping in the same bed just feels wrong."

"Listen, I will give you five thousand dollars tomorrow if you will shut up and be okay with this."

"I don't want your stupid money. I'm already getting a bunch of it," I said, annoyed. He rolled his eyes.

"Name your price."

"I don't have a price, Zane. I'm just," I fidgeted, uncomfortably. "I'm nervous."

He seemed to relax, and his eyes even softened a little. "There is no reason to be nervous. This isn't a real marriage, Ivy. I don't expect you to be a real wife in our bedroom, but it has to look completely real from the outside."

I nodded after a moment and said, "I get it."

"I'm really tired, and I'd love to get a few hours of sleep. If you come lay down, I will order an abundance of Chinese food for dinner. If you don't like Chinese, you're out of luck because they're the only ones that deliver here."

"I like Chinese," I said, sauntering to the bed. "I don't have anything to sleep in though."

He walked into the closet. I awkwardly stood beside the bed until he returned with a shirt that would reach my knees and handed it to me.

"Thanks," I said. I walked into the restroom and changed out of my jeans and stained shirt, into the shirt Zane had offered me. He knocked on the door, and when I opened it, he handed me a pair of drawstring pants.

"These are the smallest ones I could find," he said.

"They'll be fine." I quickly slipped them on and pulled the strings as far as they would go before I tied them. Zane walked past me into the restroom and shut the door.

I made my way to the giant bed. It almost looked bigger than a king-size, not that I'd ever slept in one that big.

"You're on the inside," he said from behind me. The inside of the bed meant I was to be between him and the wall.

"How wonderful." I climbed up and crawled all the way across until I reached the farthest point. Laying down, I watched Zane turn the lights off and get in as well.

Being who I am, I've been in quite a bit of awkward situations. There were times in high school that the principal called my name over the intercom more than once in a day.

I'd walked in on my Gym teacher kissing my Math teacher and not three days later saw him kissing the Spanish teacher. Gym was awkward for a good while before I finally broke the tension with a chemistry experiment. He lost his eyebrows but, I figured we were even after that.

Every situation I thought of was nothing compared to the awkwardness of laying in Zane's bed. I rolled over so I could face the wall and closed my eyes, and forcing all thoughts from my mind, I finally drifted off to sleep.

* * *

I FELT someone staring at me.

I slowly opened my eyes to see Zane laying only a foot away. He was the one staring.

"What are you looking at?" I asked.

"You," he answered. He narrowed his eyes. "You snore."

"Eh. We can't all be perfect. It runs in the family," I said, shrugging under the heavy blankets.

"You also drooled a little." He lifted his hand and pointed to a little spot on the pillow.

"I was probably dreaming about food."

"Your hair looks awful."

"Wow. Do I get to look forward to being insulted every time we wake up together? I might be a hot mess, but you are literally paying for it, so get over it."

"I was just making conversation."

I sat up in bed and glared at him. "You need to work on your conversation pieces then because you stink at it."

"We can't all be perfect," he said, throwing my words back at me.

"We can't all be perfect," I said in a mocking voice. Utterly childish, but whatever. I couldn't help it that I looked like a train wreck when I woke up. Most people looked rested after a good night's sleep; I usually looked like I got thrown into a dumpster, then after climbing out, was chased by a pack of rabid dogs into traffic where I was quickly hit by a school bus.

"I just got a text from the guy that Trina hired. He's here." Zane got out of bed and walked to the door.

"I have to get dressed first!" I yelled. He paused and looked over his shoulder.

His eyes narrowed. "You look fine." I looked down at my giant, wrinkled clothes and he added, "There's no one here you need to impress."

"I don't care about impressing anyone! I look disgusting. Just give me five minutes!"

"You don't even have any clothes," Zane reminded me. "Just come on."

"Ugh!" I smacked my forehead with the palm of my hand. "This meeting is going to be so embarrassing."

We walked down the stairs and into the kitchen where a man was sitting at the island with his back to us. He stood and turned, immediately reaching his hand out to shake Zane's.

"You must be Alessandro," Zane said.

"Yes, Sir. Good to meet you." He looked at me and nodded. No handshake. Are you kidding me?

"I'm Ivy," I said, purposefully shoving my hand out toward him. His mouth twitched before he shook my hand and introduced himself.

"Nice to meet you, Ivy, I'm Alessandro Romano, or Sandro, if you prefer."

"So, you're going to be living here?" I asked. I felt Zane's eyes on me but ignored him. This was my house now, too.

"I am."

Sandro was only a few inches shorter than Zane, but he looked equally intimidating. His dark, olive skin, dark brown eyes, and almost black hair was a massive contrast to the blue-eyed blonde I had standing beside me.

"How old are you, Sandro?" I asked. I never really liked feeling intimidated, and with these men standing in a kitchen together, well, it started to feel a little like someone trapped me in an elevator.

"Twenty-seven."

"You ever kill anyone?"

"No? Why? Did you have someone in mind?" he asked.

My eyes widened, and a grin spread across my face. "You're hired."

"I already hired him," Zane grumbled.

"Eh, details. I think I like you, Sandy," I said. The huff behind me had me rolling my eyes. I turned and wrapped my arms around my husband. "Don't worry, honey, I like you more."

A random little lady came out of the hall behind us, and I screamed. Zane's body tensed, and he tightened his arm around me.

"What are you hollering at, child?" she asked. "She" was well into her sixties and she had to be close to five feet tall. Her short curly hair was a lighter brown than my own and spotted with gray and white.

"This is Rayna, the cook," Zane said, clearing up my confusion.

"Hi," I said to her. "I didn't know anyone else was here, sorry."

"Rayna, this is Ivy." Zane introduced us, and she rushed to me and pulled me away from my husband, into a hug.

"It's so nice to meet you, sweet girl! I was so surprised when Mister Zane called me to tell me about you yesterday morning!"

"Yesterday morning?" I asked, looking over her head at him.

"Yes! Mister Zane called me and told me that he met a beautiful girl," she laughed. I looked at Zane, but his face didn't give anything away. "He said she was feisty, and he wanted to bring her home. I've worked here five years, and in that five years, I've not met a single person. I'm just so happy for you both." She wiped a tear off of her cheek.

I wrapped my arm around her shoulder and thanked her.

It made me sad to think that Zane was alone so often, and while I also wanted to be happy about him talking to Rayna about me, I reminded myself he had to sell our love story just as much as I did. Anything he said to anyone about me and our marriage was nothing short of a lie.

"I can take you now, Mister Romano," Rayna said, motioning him through the kitchen. They disappeared around the corner, and I heard their feet going up the stairs.

I gave Zane a weird look. "Why are they going upstairs?"

"The apartment entrance is up there," he said. He looked slightly uncomfortable.

"That's not awkward at all." My stomach growled as I spoke. "Can you feed me now?"

"Yeah, I'll feed you now." He walked across the kitchen and opened a drawer. Pulling out a menu, he picked up the house phone and dialed a number.

CHAPTER NINE

Zane

This was the most excitement I'd had since my exit from fame. I was in the kitchen watching my little wife shoveling food into her mouth. I'd witnessed nothing like it.

"I wish you would stop looking at me like that," she said through a mouthful of rice. I cringed.

"I wish you wouldn't talk with your mouth full," I said. She finished chewing what was in her mouth and took a long drink of soda.

"You know your mouth was hanging open? It was disgusting for me, too."

"I can assure you it was out of pure shock, not lack of manners."

She glanced up at me from her plate and said, "I was hungry, dude. How about we chill out on the insults for a while?"

I went back to paying attention to my food, and she started talking again.

"So, tell me about yourself."

"Just eat your food," I huffed.

"Why are you so grumpy?"

I made an annoyed noise, and she stopped mid-chew. "Did you just growl at me? That has to be the second or third time that's happened since we met."

"What can I say? You bring out my inner beast."

"Come on, Hubby. We've gotta learn about each other eventually. I'd rather it not be when magazines are publishing articles about us." I stared at her as I ate my egg roll. I'd hoped she'd take it as a sign that I didn't want to talk. She didn't. "Fine, I'll go first. My name is Ivy Murphy, I'm twenty-one years old, and I lived in Taylorsville from the time I turned eighteen until a couple of days ago."

"Landis," I said.

"Huh?"

"Your name is Ivy Landis."

"Right. Well, my mom and dad met in Taylorsville. My dad was an undercover cop posing as a homeless guy and Mom thought he was a pitiful mess, so she took him in. They fell in love and then got married. I'm one of seven kids."

"Are you the youngest?" I struggled to believe her parents had willingly had more children after her.

"No. I'm kid number two. Jake is the oldest by a year, and then Parker is a year younger than me. Kelly is eighteen, and then you have the twins who are thirteen and the baby, Duke, just turned twelve."

"Sounds like a circus."

"It was, but it was fun, too. I was never alone." She paused and glanced at me. "Do you have any siblings?"

"I have a younger sister named Emma. She's eighteen but still a senior in high school."

"Does she live around here?"

"They live ten minutes away."

"Who are 'they?'" she asked.

"My family."

We heard Rayna and Sandro finally coming back down the stairs.

"They were up there forever!" Ivy said under her breath.

"I'm leaving for the day, Mister Zane," Rayna said from the hall as Sandro entered the kitchen. I gave her a nod, and she quickly left.

"So, Sandy, do you like Chinese food?" Ivy asked. He quirked his lips in a half smile.

"I love Chinese food, ma'am."

Ivy scrunched her nose. "Please, call me Ivy."

"Do you think you're too young for that?" he asked.

"Not at all. It's polite, but I don't want you to call me 'ma'am' for the next five years. Ivy is my name, and that's what you should call me."

"Ivy." He nodded and smiled.

"Well, sit down, and I'll grab you some food." She stood and started looking through the cabinets. He walked to her stool and sat down, which left her without a seat.

"Tell me a little about yourself. Any family around here?" she asked.

"My dad passed away when I was a teenager, and my mom lives in Texas. No siblings." He looked at her and smile. "Anything specific you want to know?"

"Favorite food?"

"Birthday cake. You?"

She laughed. "Pizza. Favorite color?"

"Green."

"Me, too! Favorite movie?"

"Any action movie is good in my book. Let me guess; you're a romance junkie?"

I was feeling like a third wheel in my own house, and I didn't like it.

Ivy moved to stand between Sandro and me, placing his plate in front of him, and I acted on impulse; I grabbed her and pulled her up onto my lap. Sandro wasn't paying any attention to us, and I was thankful because she gave me a questioning look. I shrugged my shoulders and pulled her plate closer to her. I wasn't about to vocalize the fact that I was jealous.

"I like romance," she said.

"I pegged you for the type."

"What does having a bodyguard mean?" She turned her head to look at me, putting her only a couple of inches away. I didn't like the camaraderie she already shared with the man I was paying to protect her; I couldn't help it, so I leaned in and softly kissed the corner of her mouth. "It means we're going to protect you from harm."

Her eyes were enormous and confused. I couldn't blame her. She shifted slightly on my lap and went back to eating her food, accepting the answer I gave.

"Do you guys have any plans tonight?" Sandro asked.

"No," I answered immediately.

"I'd like to go look around the city," Ivy threw a sharp look over her shoulder. This woman should have had a sign that said, 'Beware, I test patience.'

"Tomorrow. It's getting late," I said.

"But we just woke up!"

"I wouldn't mind taking you out tonight," Sandro butted in.

"Okay! Let's go!" She was excited.

I leaned in close to her ear to remind her of her problem. "You don't have any clothes."

"I'll wear my dirty ones. I don't even care!"

"We'll go tomorrow when your things get here." I put force behind my words, letting her know what I said was final.

Her body stiffened for a moment before she took another bite of her food and slid down off my lap. Placing her plate in the sink, she looked at Sandro and tried to smile. "It was nice to meet you. I look forward to you following me around everywhere." Her attitude was as evident as her sarcasm. "Goodnight."

"Goodnight," he called out as she left the kitchen. When she left, he chuckled under his breath. "She's going to be a handful."

Instead of responding, I stood and left before I did something that I would regret.

When I walked into our bedroom, Ivy was sitting on her side of the bed looking sadly at her phone. I felt guilty again. I couldn't explain it to her, but I wasn't ready for her to leave the house without me yet. We'd been married less than twenty-four hours, and I wasn't sure if she would bail on me.

"We'll go out tomorrow," I said, drawing her attention away from her phone.

"Okay." She sounded defeated.

"Why are you still so upset?"

"It's not that. It's my dad. I've been texting him a little bit, and he's pretty ticked off at me. Understandable, but it's still just as crushing."

I sat on the bed beside her. "I'm sure he'll get over it, eventually."

"It's not that simple. My dad has always been the parent that laughed with me when I did something crazy. Mom always worried, but Dad thought I was funny. I know this is a completely different situation, but he's barely talking to me. I hurt him, and I hate this feeling." A tear slid down her cheek and onto her chin.

"I think it's going to be okay." I slowly reached over and wiped her tear away.

"I hope so. Could I invite my parents to come meet you?"

"If you're sure I won't wind up dead in the woods somewhere, then yeah, I think that would be great."

"Really?" She sat up a little straighter.

"This is your home now, of course you can invite your family."

Her phone started ringing, and the smile she gave the screen was the most beautiful smile I think I'd ever seen in my life. For a split second, I wanted to be the person that put that look on her face.

"Hi, Cal!" I glanced at the screen and saw a guy around my age, with a shaved head, looking back at her with a huge grin.

"What's up, Buttercup?"

"I heard about your knee. How are you doing?"

"I'm on some serious painkillers, so I'm doing pretty stellar right now," he laughed. Who the heck was this guy?

"You look extremely happy for a guy with a busted kneecap."

"I am. So, I hear congratulations are in order." He gave her a knowing grin that I didn't understand.

"Thank you," she whispered.

"Where's your husband?"

She turned the phone sideways so the guy could see me. His goofy grin returned, and he waved.

"I'm Cal!" he yelled.

"Cal! He can hear you just fine."

"Oh, sorry!" he laughed. "What's your name? My dad keeps calling you 'That Evil Man, ' but I'm going out on a limb here and thinking that's not it."

"Zane," I replied.

"Welcome to the family, Zane." I looked at Ivy in confusion.

"He's my cousin," she said, and I nodded. "I'm gonna go, Cal. Go get some rest and text me tomorrow."

"Alright. G'night, cousin," he said. "Bye, Zane."

"He's an idiot," she said, but she was smiling, so I didn't think she meant it insultingly. He made her happy. "Do you think we should take a selfie and put it on our phones?"

"Why would we do that?" I stood and pulled my shirt off, throwing it in the basket in the corner of the room.

"Well, this is all for your publicity; so I can update my social media and stuff. I mean, no one's going to know we're married." She looked up, and her eyes widened. "That's a lot of ink."

"You're going to put a picture of us on all your social media accounts?" I asked.

"That's what I just said ... " She was staring at my shoulders.

"Alright." I got back into bed and scooted back until I was against the headboard. "Come here."

She moved to sit beside me, but I caught her before she got comfortable and pulled her over until she was seated in-between my legs. "Lean back," I said.

"Uh, smile." She sounded nervous. I pulled my mouth into a convincingly happy look, and she snapped the picture, then turned the camera around. We looked stupid. Her eyes conveyed her nerves, and I just looked like the jerk sitting behind her. I wrapped my arms around her.

"You've gotta relax, Ivy. If this is going out into the internet world, it has to be convincing."

"I know, this is just so weird."

"Close your eyes and just chill for a minute." She took a deep breath and rested her head on my shoulder. I looked down at her face to see her eyes closed and she was beet red.

"You said you have six siblings?" I asked, trying to get her to feel more comfortable.

"Yeah," she smiled. "Murphy kids are the greatest."

"I bet you've missed them, living so far away."

"I have. I felt guilty for leaving them when I first moved to Taylorsville, but I just felt like I had to get away. I want to see the world, you know?"

"When I first moved away I felt guilty, too," I said. She looked up at me in question, and I gave her a sad smile. "I felt bad for leaving my mom and sister."

"You came back." It wasn't a question.

"I did." She smiled her beautiful smile at me and opened the camera on the phone. I didn't know what it was that made her finally relax, but when we looked at the second picture she took, we both seemed truly happy.

CHAPTER TEN

Ivy

Was it wrong that I thought my husband was hot? I liked to think not. I mean, sure, I didn't know the guy, but he was still technically my husband. Not appreciating the view seemed like a waste of gorgeous.

When I looked up, and he had his shirt off, I slightly freaked out. His tattoos covered his broad shoulders and his chest and back. The ink stopped a little ways above where a shirt sleeve would. Which was why I had no idea he'd had any.

I was still sitting between his legs, with my back pressed against his chest, while we looked at the picture we'd taken. We looked convincing. The moment he said he'd come back to this place just to be near his mom and sister, I immediately relaxed in his arms. It reminded me of what my mom always told my sisters and me when we were growing up.

"Marry a man who treats his mom like gold," she'd said, and she told the boys to be men that would make a woman proud. They didn't have to be strong and tough, but they had to be kind.

When Zane talked about his mom and sister, his voice was tender, loving even. It was as if he couldn't be harsh when speaking of them, even if he tried. I couldn't wait to meet them if they caused this change in him.

"I guess I should get on everything and update it," I said after a few minutes of silence.

"That's a good idea."

I logged into an account and updated my profile picture, then I edited my personal information to married.

"Do you have an account?" I asked.

"Yeah, but Trina runs it. She runs all my social media."

Strange.

"Maybe we could do a live video on your page."

"Yeah, I'll get my login stuff from her tomorrow."

"Oh, wow! I already have a comment." I clicked on the update, and sure enough, it was from my older brother, Jake.

'You look happy, baby sister. Congrats.'

"Who's that?" Zane asked.

"My brother," I answered. "He's the oldest." I replied to Jake and turned the screen off.

"I need to call my grandpa," I sighed.

"Now?"

"Yeah. I haven't spoken to him since I left work." I stopped mid-sentence and looked at Zane. "Did we really only get married this morning?"

He nodded, and I tried to wrap my head around the crazy day I'd had. In less than forty-two hours; I'd met Zane, gotten engaged and married. I met my bodyguard, who seemed rather pleasant, let a lady I didn't know hug me, visited Las Vegas and was now living with my husband in Denver, Colorado. I mean, wow!

Suddenly, a conversation with Pop seemed like the least intimidating thing I'd face.

I sat up and climbed over Zane's leg to get off the bed. Walking into the restroom, I shut the door and sat on the edge of the tub. I dialed the number and prayed he answered.

"Ivy." Pop's gruff voice came over the line and held so much disappointment.

"Hey, Pop."

There was silence on the other end that held a command. My grandfather wanted an explanation.

"I am so sorry I ran off. I wanted to tell you, but I was afraid you would try to stop me. Being married to Zane is what I want. I'm happy and safe, and I know that's not a good enough explanation. I know saying sorry and being happy doesn't make it okay, but I hope that in time, you can forgive me. I want you to come here and see the house and really meet Zane. I know you'll like him. Well, eventually."

"Do you know anything about him, do you positively know him?" he asked.

"I know he got involved in some horrible things when he was younger, but he got the help he needed. We're supposed to give people second chances and believe in them. That's what you all have taught me. I mean, you let mom move a homeless guy into her apartment. I know he was a cop and all, but you didn't know that!"

"I'm going to tell you a secret, and I want you to promise me you will never tell a soul. Okay?"

"Okay," I whispered.

"I knew who your dad was long before he told me."

I felt my heart pick up speed at his confession. "What? There's no way. He was undercover!"

"I never stopped checking up on him, even after he got adopted. I knew when he transferred to narcotics. I went to school with the Chief that was over the operation at the time when your dad went undercover."

"I still don't understand how you knew it was him. It's not like they told you."

"I knew what he looked like and when I saw him, I called Richard and we talked. Of course, he couldn't tell me details, but he told me that Brennan was going to be unavailable for a while. I'm not stupid."

"Wow! This is crazy. No wonder you let him into mom's life so easily."

"Now, don't go acting like it was easy. I was losing my baby girl to a man she didn't truly know. I couldn't tell her because I couldn't risk his assignment, but I tried to be a voice of reason when I could. Heck of a lot of good that did since she went and married him." He sounded a little put-off, and I laughed. I knew Pop loved my dad like he was his own son. My grandparents lucked out with really great kids. I just hoped my parents felt the same way about theirs.

"I hope you know I love you and I want you to be happy," he said. "I was so scared that we'd done something to run you off."

"You could never run me off," I said, tears had collected in my eyes. "I love you and Gram so much! I should have told you guys."

"It's over and done with now," he sighed. "Unfortunately, you'll have to deal with the consequences of being married. It's not all fun and games. Marriage is the biggest decision you could ever make for your life outside of becoming a parent. I was in a loveless marriage, and the only good thing that came out of it was your mother."

"I know it was a big decision. I promise, it'll all be okay though."

"Well, squirt, I should probably go help your grandma make some dinner. She gets upset if I sit around and make her wait on me hand and foot."

"Okay," I laughed. "Tell Gram I love her, and I love you, Pop."

"I love you, too," he said. "I'm not okay with how this happened, but I'll never stop loving you."

"I know," I replied. We disconnected, and I walked back into the bedroom. Putting the phone on the nightstand, I climbed up onto the bed and over to my spot.

"So, I've got a question for you," I said to Zane as I got under the covers. He looked at me, and I assumed that meant I could continue. "Where are we going on our honeymoon?"

His eyes widened. "What are you talking about, Ivy? We're not going anywhere."

"Yes. We are." My voice should have left no room for argument, but of course, that wasn't Zane's way.

"No, we are not."

"Listen, Buddy, you promised me adventure, and that's what you're going to give me!"

"You can demand whatever your little heart desires. You can ask until you're blue in the face, but we aren't going on a honeymoon." He was getting irritated.

Well, forget him!

"Hand me my phone." He looked at the phone, then back at me.

"Why?" he asked, rightfully suspicious.

"I'm going to post updates about how sucky of a husband you are!"

"You can't do that."

"Oh, yes, I can!"

"This is like blackmail. You can't act like you're going to drag my name through the mud and hold it over my head whenever you want something."

"I'm not trying to be that way, but Zane, you promised me adventure. You can't act like you didn't, because you did, and I want to go somewhere. It doesn't have to be anywhere fancy, but I'd love to go somewhere nice. I want to see stuff. Like, the Grand Canyon or maybe a black sand beach. It's not fair that you marry me and then break your promises."

He ran his hands roughly over his face and made the sound that he'd made in the kitchen.

"I'll think about it."

I sighed. That was as good of an answer as I was going to get tonight. "Thank you."

"I'm going to need to go on medication for my stomach," he grumbled.

"Is that ulcer acting up again?" I laughed.

"I'm turning the television on now, and I want you to not talk for at least an hour. I need a break from your level of crazy."

"We got married less than twenty-four hours ago, and you already need a break? If that's the case, I don't see this working out." I was only joking, but he looked at me with complete hurt and shock battling in his eyes.

"Don't say that. I need this to work more than anything, so if you're just going to mess around and not take it seriously, then you should have told me a long time ago."

"I was just kidding," I said, feeling bad for freaking him

out. "I promised you the next five years of my life. I don't intend on breaking any of my promises to you. Ever."

He looked into my eyes for a moment and took a reassuring breath. "Okay. Then I'll make sure I never break any promises I've made to you, in return. Tomorrow, figure out where you want to go, and we'll go on a real honeymoon. We'll go somewhere for a couple of weeks."

"Really?" I squealed.

"I don't make it a habit of needing people. I would prefer to never rely on anyone other than myself, but I need you. I need you to invest in me for the few years of your life. That's an insane thing to ask a stranger, but if you invest in me, I'll do the same for you."

At that moment I experienced happiness so overwhelming it was hard to breathe. My smile was so broad I probably looked crazy, but I didn't care. I flung myself at Zane and hugged him as well I could in the bed, and when he wrapped an arm around me, he said, "We're in this together."

"Together," I repeated.

When Zane turned the lights off and started the movie, I tried and failed to pay attention. I'd heard the expression 'hot and cold' before, but this was the first time I could apply it to something in my life.

Zane was a mystery to me. One minute, he was completely closed off and even aggressive to a certain extent, but then the next thing I knew, he showed vulnerability. But, I guess you can't have all the answers to the questions you have about someone in such a short amount of time.

After the way the last two days had gone, it surprised me I was still up and running. It felt kind of like a dream, to be honest. Like I was floating outside my body and watching all of these things happen to someone else.

I'd never decided how I felt about getting married. I knew I wanted to have my own family someday, but never in my wildest dreams did I think I'd get married at twenty-one. Granted, this wasn't a real relationship, it was still pretty weird. I felt like I had to keep reminding myself that I had a husband, like when Zane told me that my last name wasn't Murphy anymore.

Marriage was so far off the list of things I'd wanted to accomplish; the name change hadn't even occurred to me.

CHAPTER ELEVEN

Ivy

When I woke up the next morning-day two of being Mrs. Ivy Landis, I noticed Zane's hold on my arm. I laid still for as long as I could, trying not to disturb his sleep, and studied him.

Eventually, I couldn't hold still anymore. I moved my arm out of his grasp and sat up in bed.

"Where are you going?" Zane's voice was husky from sleep, and I moved out of his reach toward the foot of the bed.

"I'm going to the bathroom. I didn't realize I needed permission to get out of bed."

"You don't."

"Then why did I wake up with your hand wrapped around my arm for the second morning in a row?"

He stared at me for a moment before sitting up. He ran

his hand over his head and sighed. "I'm sorry. I didn't realize I was even touching you in my sleep. I promised you that you were safe, and I've made you feel the opposite."

I moved toward the head of the bed where Zane rested against the headboard. I was close enough that our legs touched when I placed my hand on his cheek, forcing him to look at me.

"I'm not going anywhere. I'm here of my own free will, and I'm not going to abandon you. We're in this together, remember?" I let my hand drop to my lap. "It's like you're scared I'm going to run away and I guess I want to understand why that is."

As soon as I uttered the words, I knew I wouldn't get a full answer, but I had hoped. Regret colored his features before everything I was hoping for shut down. Before my very eyes, he'd gone from open and willing to talk to a closed off robot.

"I'm sorry that I scared you by holding onto you. I'll try not to let it happen again, but I was asleep when I did it, so I wasn't aware it happened."

I felt my shoulders sag when I nodded. Zane quickly got out of bed and shut himself in the restroom before turning on the shower.

Day-two down. I pulled up the calculator on my phone and typed in some numbers before I let out a groan.

One thousand, eight hundred and twenty-four days to go, with the leap year next year.

What on earth had I done?

I walked downstairs and prepared breakfast while Zane got dressed. I decided my new goal in life was going to be trying to convince him that not everyone would abandon him, and before I knew it, we were sitting at the island together. I hadn't seen Sandro all morning, but I figured he was still getting settled into the apartment.

"Is there anywhere you want to go?" I asked Zane.

"I said you could choose where we go," he answered. His phone alerted him to a message, and he read it before saying, "Looks like your stuff is here."

"Oh, man! I don't know if I've ever been more excited about something." I stood and rushed to the door to open it. Sure enough, there was an older gentleman parked in the driveway. I walked out to greet him.

"Thank you for driving this here," I said. I noticed the other car parked on the road with someone in the driver's seat.

"That's my job, ma'am." He was quickly glancing between me and something behind me. "Here are the keys. You have a nice day."

"Wait, don't I have to pay you?" I hollered after him, but he ignored me.

I turned to see what could have scared him off and noticed a shirtless Zane with his arms crossed over his chest. "Of course," I whispered.

He helped me carry all my things into our room, and I started unloading everything.

"These are your drawers," Zane said, pointing to a dresser in the closet. He picked up one of my t-shirts and put it on a hanger before hanging it up. I surpassed a laugh.

"Thanks for helping," I said when we finished. I zipped my suitcases up and placed them beside my new dresser. All I had left was my toiletry bag, and I didn't want his help with that.

"Not a problem," he replied.

"So, about the honeymoon, I think I either want to go to Hawaii or Alaska."

"Those are pretty different places, Wife," he smirked.

"I know, but both are equally interesting, in my opinion, husband." What a jerk. He walked to the bed and sat down.

"If you say so."

"Where would you go if you could go anywhere?" I sat on the bed beside him and noticed he was flipping through emails on his phone.

"Hawaii is fun if you go to the right places. I think you'd enjoy it." He glanced over at me and gave me a half smile that didn't reach his eyes.

"Is Sandro going with us?" The smile disappeared.

"No." He didn't seem to like that question.

"I'll only have you to protect me?" I laughed.

"You think that's funny?"

"No way! You're scary." I was honest, but I couldn't help my smile. I noticed his cheeks twitch in response.

"I don't think you're scared of me, Ivy, and that is just something I'm going to have to fix." He stood and moved directly in front of me. Grabbing me under the arms, he threw me on the bed and climbed on with me.

"I can't help it!" I laughed. I may have been laughing, but his sudden change in behavior made me a little nervous. If it weren't for the grin on his face that caused the butterfly feeling in my stomach, I would have tried to sit up or something, but his mood froze me in place. He sat on my legs and grabbed my arms, holding them above my head with one hand.

"So," he said, showing off perfect, straight white teeth. "Where are you most ticklish?"

My eyes widened in horror. "You can't tickle me! I'll pee or something crazy!"

"Is it here?" he asked, pointing to the place between my neck and shoulder. "No, I don't think that's it."

His finger slowly moved from right below my ear, across my neck, to the other side. "Here?" he asked and then shook his head. "No, I think I know the most likely place."

He moved his large hand to my ribs and gently squeezed. I tried as hard as I could not to give it away, but it was impossible. I flinched and let out a small squeak. He squeezed a little harder, and a genuine laugh escaped me.

"Please don't do this!" I begged. I didn't want to embarrass myself.

"I think it's the only way I can instill fear in you, Ivy. I can't look like a weakling."

All of a sudden, he released my arms and grabbed my sides with both hands. I started laughing as I grabbed onto his wrists, failing to pull them away. I squirmed and twisted, trying to get free, but it was hopeless. Tears were running down the side of my face and into my hair, and I could barely hear his deep chuckle over my laughter. It felt like the torture went on forever.

"Okay!" I screamed. "You're the scariest man in the entire world!"

He paused to stare into my eyes. His smile was still present and so large that his eyes crinkled in the corners. "Swear it."

"I swear."

His eyes moved to my lips then slowly made their way back to my eyes before his smile faded and he proceeded to get off the bed. "You don't ever have to worry about anything when you're with me. I'll keep you safe," he said before walking out of the room.

"What in the world?" I asked myself. My breathing was erratic and my sides and stomach ached from the amount of laughter that had escaped me.

I got up and moved to the closet to pick out an outfit for the day before locking myself in the bathroom.

After I showered and dressed in my clean clothes, I went in search of Zane but found a young girl I hadn't met standing in the laundry room.

"Oh, sorry. I was looking for Zane." She pursed her lips and tossed her long, blonde hair over her shoulder.

"You're his new wife?" she asked with a sour expression.

"That'd be me. I'm Ivy." I extended my hand in greeting, but she looked at it and scoffed. "You must be Zariah."

"That's right, Miss Ivy," Rayna said from behind me. I jumped, and she laughed under her breath. I moved to allow her in with a small basket of kitchen towels. "She doesn't like you because she says she is in love with Mister Zane."

Zariah's face turned a deep red, and she wore a shocked expression. She couldn't believe Rayna had outed her, I assumed. I guess the appropriate reaction would have been to stake my claim, but all I could think was how unfortunate it was that she was attracted to such a turd. Sure, he was hot, but dealing with his attitude was kind of like eating a spoon full of garlic powder; it left a horrible taste in your mouth for days.

"He is quite a catch," I said, instead of playing the jealous wife. She shot me a questioning look, so I shrugged. "It was nice to meet you, Zariah, but I'll let you ladies get back to work. Let me know if I can help at all."

I left them to their tasks and ventured into the basement.

I checked Zane's office and found him sitting on the couch, reading a book.

"Can we leave for Hawaii soon?" I asked as soon as I stepped through the door. He looked up from his book.

"How soon?"

"Yesterday?" I joked.

"We can leave whenever you want. This will work out great because Trina set an interview up with Celebrity Glamour Magazine in a little over a month from now. Do you think we should have pictures of the honeymoon hanging in our living room? I think that's what people are supposed to do."

"Well, my parents have pictures of the two of them everywhere in the house. I'm pretty sure if a stranger walked in, they'd know my parents loved each other just by the pictures, so it sounds like a solid idea to me."

"That's the plan, then. We'll just have to make sure to take a bunch of pictures while we're on our trip."

"Here's the problem," I said. "I don't think I'll have a problem looking in love because I'll be so excited about being somewhere I've never been, but you don't seem like the type to let loose and smile a bunch."

"What's your point?"

"No one is going to believe you're in love with me if you're so grumpy all the time! Love does things to people. It makes them feel light and fluffy. Ya know?"

"Not at all."

I pinched the bridge of my nose and prayed for patience. "This is impossible."

"I think it will be fine, Ivy," he huffed. "Let's book a flight while you're down here."

We walked to his desk, and I stood beside his chair while he got online.

"Can we leave tomorrow?" I asked.

"I thought you wanted to tour Denver? If we leave tomorrow, we have to pack today."

"I can see Denver whenever since I live here now."

"Okay. Let's go pack. There's a flight tomorrow afternoon."

I won't lie, I screamed while I ran upstairs to pack my belongings up even though I'd spent the morning doing the opposite.

CHAPTER TWELVE

Zane

Ivy slept the entire flight to Hawaii and went to bed as soon as we landed because of her headache. I didn't even know humans could sleep that long. The minute she woke up the following morning she wanted to go to the beach, and when we arrived, she started playing in the water. Like a little kid.

She was running and jumping over waves, without going into the water past her knees, and I don't know what came over me, but I laughed at her. She was adorable in her teal and white bathing suit, her giant floppy hat and sunglasses that took up half of her face.

I noticed the man with the camera too late. He was sitting far enough away to seem inconspicuous, but too close for my comfort. I wanted to feel irritated that he was going to force me to play the doting husband, but I couldn't find any anger inside me. I wanted to get in the ocean and be goofy with this crazy girl.

"You decided to join me?" She removed her sunglasses and grinned up at me when I approached.

"We have company," I said, nodding to the left where I'd left the cameraman on the beach. Her smile told me she understood what I meant and when she leaned up to kiss me, I didn't hesitate.

When we broke apart, something in her expression had changed. She looked so vulnerable under her flushed cheeks and wide eyes.

"Are you okay?" I asked, running my thumb over the light color on her cheek.

"I'm okay," she smiled. "Let's play."

"Ten minutes, and then we need to go eat. You slept through breakfast, and I don't want you to pass out in the water or something. I don't know CPR."

"How could you not know CPR? It's in about a million movies."

I shrugged. "I don't ever pay attention."

"You should learn. It could come in handy one day."

"You're the only one I'm worried about keeping alive for the next few years, so just don't get into a situation where I need to know how to do it," I said it jokingly but was shocked by how much the thought of something happening to her scared me.

The revelation of how much I truly needed her scared me.

"Promise me," I urged, even though I wasn't sure what I was asking her to promise.

"I promise," she answered without hesitation.

* * *

WE WERE EATING lunch in our hotel room when Trina called to inform us that we'd made headline news. The man on the beach had sold our picture the minute he got a chance. It surprised me anyone knew who I was anymore, to be honest. No one had paid much attention to my life lately, and I was almost nervous about what the gossip articles might say. I felt the need to warn Ivy again, but she shrugged it off. I couldn't convince her that she was crazy for marrying me. I honestly don't know why I was trying to make her realize it. Maybe I was preparing myself for the inevitable. There was no way she'd stay with me for five years. My demons were much too dark for her.

"What are we going to do now?" she asked.

"Want to go swim with sharks?"

"No!"

Why did Ivy's laugh make me smile? I picked up her empty plate and sat the dirty dishes on the cart room service brought up before sitting on the love seat beside Ivy. The hotel room resembled an apartment more than a hotel, and she loved it.

"We have to do something neither of us has ever done."

"I've never been to Hawaii, so I think that should count!"

"It doesn't. Let's go, snorkeling."

"That doesn't sound fun." I saw the look of fear on her face before she could hide it.

"Are you scared of something?" I teased. She married a stranger in less than twenty-four hours, so in my eyes, she was fearless. I felt like snorkeling shouldn't hold a candle to that.

"What if a shark comes out of nowhere and bites me?"

I couldn't help but laugh. While it was completely understandable why it would scare her, I just couldn't take it seriously. I laughed because she married one monster, and she was afraid to swim with another.

I moved closer to her on the seat and threw my arm over the back. Her head fell back against my arm, and she looked up at me with the question still lingering.

"If I see a shark coming toward you, I'll punch it in the face for you, and I'll swim slower than you, in case it's starving."

Her eyes widened. "I don't want you to die!"

"Come on, babe. If we aren't going in the water, then we're going to go shop." I picked her up and threw her over my shoulder. After grabbing my wallet and Ivy's hat, I walked out the door and toward the main road.

Our hotel was close to a whole strip of touristy stores where lots of people would be roaming around. The thought annoyed me.

"You can put me down now," she said from behind me. I smiled and sat her on her feet.

"I forgot you were up there."

"Right!" she laughed and adjusted her dress. She'd called it a summer dress, but it looked like a regular one to me. "Are you looking for something specific?"

"I figured we could get souvenirs for our families."

"Really?"

"Really. Pick out whatever."

She turned to run off, but I quickly grabbed her hand. "We have to stay together."

"Sorry, I got excited." The light was still in her eyes. At this point, I wasn't sure if it ever actually went away.

"Who all are you going to buy something for?" she asked

as we approached the first store.

"My mom and my sister," I answered.

"Can we get something for Zariah and Rayna, too?"

"If you want to."

We walked into a store, and Ivy started picking things up right away. After a few minutes, she started handing everything to me, so I could help her carry it and the smile on my face became permanent.

"There are lots of other stores," I reminded her.

"I forgot." She inspected the pile in my hands. "I guess this will do for the first store then."

"I created a monster," I said under my breath, but she heard me.

She looked up at me and smiled. "You did."

"When we get back home, you'll have a debit card. You'll be able to buy whatever you want whenever you want."

"You shouldn't say things like that out loud. Someone might steal from you," she whispered.

We made our way to the cashier and paid for our things, then went to the next store.

"Would you mind picking something out for my mom and sister? You're a girl and probably know what they'd like better."

"First of all, I'm a woman. Second of all, I already picked out their gifts. They're in the bags you're carrying."

We shopped for what seemed like hours and when we got back to the hotel room, and I looked at the time, I realized it had been four hours to be exact. We had thirteen bags full of trinkets, shirts, and who knows what else. Ivy's phone rang, and she took it to the bathroom to answer. As soon as she shut the door, I quietly followed and listened.

"Hello?" There was a moment of silence before she said,

"Are you still mad at me?"

I figured it was probably her parents, so I walked away and left her alone. I started pulling things out of the bags and tried to figure out which items belonged to who. When Ivy finally came out of the bathroom, she started helping me, and she had things sorted into fifteen piles.

"Who all did you buy things for?" I asked.

"My parents, siblings, grandparents, your mom and sister, Zariah, Rayna, and Sandro."

"Sandro?" My mood quickly shifted to irritation.

"Yes? He works for you, too. I couldn't get two members of your staff something without getting him something as well. It's rude."

"Whatever," I said, before grabbing my clothes and walking into the bathroom. I slammed the door and got into the shower.

I told myself I was mad because she was going to make it look like she had a crush on her bodyguard. I went as far as to say to myself she was going to ruin this whole thing for me, but the truth was it irritated me that she hadn't picked something out for me.

How irrational was that? I could buy whatever I wanted, and it upset me that my wife of a few days hadn't picked a few dollars' gift out for me. I was stupid.

"Zane?" Ivy's voice inside the bathroom startled me. I hadn't heard the door open, so I wasn't sure how long she'd been standing there.

"What?"

"Are you mad at me?"

I took a deep breath and exhaled slowly. "No. I'm not mad at you."

"Then what's wrong?"

"Nothing's wrong. I just really needed a shower, and I'm hungry," I answered.

"I can run down and get us something to eat," she offered.

"No, don't go without me. I don't want you to get lost." I couldn't see her, but I knew she rolled her eyes at my statement. "And don't roll your eyes at me."

"How did you-."

"Go get dressed up and we'll go to a nice place for dinner." I hesitated a moment before quietly adding, "If that's something you'd like to do."

"You are so weird," she said before shutting the door.

I wasn't the only weird one. When I walked out of the bathroom, Ivy was laying across the bed, so her head was hanging off it. She was spraying hairspray into her hair and shaking her head like crazy.

"What in the world are you doing?" I asked.

"I needed some volume, and I get dizzy if I stand and do this," she answered like it was obvious. When she stood and fixed her hair, I noticed she'd put makeup on and lined her eyes in black. "Do I look better with or without the makeup?" she asked, looking into the mirror.

"Honestly, you look beautiful either way," I said, and she smiled.

We walked to a nice restaurant that had a beach view. The sun was setting, and musicians were playing in the front. After taking our seats, the hostess handed us each a menu.

"I love it here," Ivy said after we ordered.

"The restaurant?"

Her lips quirked up on the side. "That, too, so far, but I enjoy being here in Hawaii."

I nodded. "It's nice, but it's not like being at home."

"Do you spend a lot of time at home?" she asked. A few

couples had stood and started dancing to the romantic-sounding music the band was playing.

"I spend almost all my time at home unless I meet with Trina. I've not had a reason to get out of the house in a while," I said after the waitress sat our plates on the table.

"Does it make you sad?"

"Why would it make me sad?"

"I mean, did you go out a lot before?"

"Oh," I hesitated. "I went out too much. It's what got me where I'm currently at in life. Everything just went to my head, and I lost who I was. Thankfully, Trina was there to control my finances, or I would have lost absolutely everything."

"She seems to care about you."

I didn't respond.

"Let's go dance," I said when she finished eating. I stood and grabbed her hand, pulling her to the dance floor. She placed her hands on my shoulders, and I put mine around her waist.

"Don't step on my toes," I joked. I wanted to see Ivy smile, and I got what I was after.

"I'd barely hurt you if I did. You better not step on mine, though."

"Two years of dance class taught me better than that." The confession surprised her.

"Dance class?"

I gently pushed her body away from me and held her hand. I twirled her twice before bringing her flush against me and holding on tight. Her eyes were wide with shock, but she was smiling.

Without saying another word, I pulled her arms up around my neck, and she rested her head on my chest.

97

CHAPTER THIRTEEN

Ivy

My first thought upon waking up was, are you kidding me?

Zane's hand gripped my shirt, and that was the last straw for me. I felt like we'd had a great evening and I hadn't given him a single reason to suspect I would leave. I was horrible with direction, so I had no faith in my ability to find the restaurant from the night before, let alone the airport. I had no access to money. As far as I was concerned, Zane had kept his word to me, so I had every intention of keeping my promises to him. We were finally becoming friends, and he was making my dream come true. I didn't understand why he thought I'd leave after he did something so special for me.

I needed to make a point, to prove he could trust me.

When I finally succeeded in removing his grasp, I stood slowly and went to the restroom.

I thought about going to the beach alone, just to show him I wasn't going anywhere, even if he wasn't watching me. I wanted him to trust me, but I figured going that far would only do the opposite. Instead, I dialed room service and ordered breakfast for the two of us. When it arrived, I opened the sliding glass doors that led outside and placed the food on the table that sat on the sand. I looked over my shoulder to the sleeping man I'd left in the bed and smiled to myself.

I walked over to the bed and touched his shoulder. "Zane?" He didn't even twitch.

I tried again. "Wake up, sleepyhead."

He grunted, and I grinned. "What do you want, Ivy?"

"I want you to wake up and come eat breakfast with me."

He finally opened his eyes and looked at me. His eyebrows drew together, and he glanced at the open doors, then back at me.

"How long have you been awake?" he asked. I rolled my eyes at his silly question. No, not silly. I rolled my eyes at his stupid question.

"Zane, you don't have to act like you're holding me as a prisoner. I married you, came to Hawaii with you, and I'm going to be beside you for the next five years. I don't know what it's going to take to make you believe me, but I refuse to live with your fear of me leaving. Don't make your issues become issues in our marriage and friendship." I paused when he looked away. "Please believe that I'm not going anywhere unless you physically hurt me; which I believe you would never do, so it's not something we have to worry about."

He finally made eye contact again. "I don't trust people."

"I'm not just some random person anymore, Zane. I'm your wife, and if you really can't see that, then our marriage is going to be a giant battle. Is it such a bad thing to have at least a little bit of trust between us?"

He sighed, and I left the subject alone for now. "Let's just go eat breakfast, okay?" I offered him my hand, and he surprised me when he took it and stood with me. We walked outside and sat down at the table.

"I called room service," I said before he could worry about if I'd left the room. He nodded and started eating his bacon.

As we ate, I listened to the ocean waves in the distance, crashing against the beach. I decided I was in love with this place. This entire moment. Even with my broody husband, I didn't think I could ever forget a single second of this trip. A memory surfaced from when I was a little girl and would listen to Pop tell stories of the placed he'd had to go during his time in the military. They had stationed him near a beach at one point, but he hated the salt in the water and how the sand ended up everywhere when you finally left. It always made me laugh when he'd end the story with a shudder, but secretly I felt a little envious. I wanted to visit the beach and take it with me when I left. And now, here I was.

"What are the plans for the day?" he asked after a few minutes.

"I thought maybe we could spend the day on the beach. I know it's stupid, but I want to go read and just relax."

"You had me bring you to Hawaii so you could sit and read a book?"

"Yep!" I answered cheerfully.

"Whatever you want, Princess." I looked up to see him smiling at me, and I arched my eyebrow.

"Princess? Really? I think you're the one who has a royal complex. Mr. I-Need-An-Entire-King-Size-Comforter-All-To-Myself. You leave me with the simple cover sheet every night!" I said, laughing.

"You're going to have to learn to put up a fight then." He

finished drinking his coffee and stood. "Let's change and get our stuff together. I think my body knows it's about to get some vitamin D because I feel like I'm actually looking forward to spending the day in the sun."

"Well, Pale Legs, from looking at you, I'd say you're due for quite a few days in the sun."

"What did you just call me?" He stopped in the doorway so I couldn't get past.

"Pale legs," I repeated.

"Do we need to repeat my scare tactics? I just don't think you understand that I will tickle you until you pee in your weird little green and purple shorts and I don't even care."

I looked down at my shorts. "These aren't weird! They're purple shorts with little green dinosaurs. What's wrong with that?"

"They look like they belong to a child."

"Well," I tried recalling where I'd bought them. "I'm pretty sure I did get them in the youth section of a clothing store."

"You're changing the subject Mrs. Landis." His use of my name forced my eyes to his without my permission. He was inching closer to me, and I got the impression I needed to do something. I needed to do something like run and I needed to do it quickly.

I turned and bolted toward the water, but I wasn't fast enough. Zane grabbed me by the waist from behind and swung me around. I let out a combination of a scream and laughter, which I didn't even know was possible until I met him.

"Stop!" I laughed while he twirled faster and faster. It was almost more torture than being tickled. I closed my eyes and tried to breathe, but it was nearly impossible. I was going to pass out from holding my breath, or Zane was going to drop me and knock me out.

Thankfully, depending on how you looked at it, Zane lost his balance, and we fell together. Somehow, my elbow made contact with his nose while his knee ended up in my spine.

I almost threw up from the combination of dizziness and pain.

"Are you okay?" he asked. I looked up and gasped in horror. Blood covered his entire face.

"Your face!" I yelled.

"You know how to make a man feel good about his looks," he laughed, but then cringed when he wiped his face with his shirt.

"I'm so sorry!" I said, trying to stand. He helped me up, and I winced as I straightened my back.

Ouch.

"Let me see." He walked behind me and lifted my shirt to see where his knee made contact. "Well, that's going to be a bruise. I'm sorry. I lost my footing in the sand and couldn't stop the fall."

I couldn't help but laugh, which made me wince again. "We're hopeless." I looked up and saw fresh blood under Zane's nose. "Let's go get your face cleaned up."

"We should get an ice pack on your back, too."

When we were both cleaned up, changed, and armed with one ice pack each, we made our way to the beach with our bags.

I spread my towel out and laid on my stomach, so I could rest the ice on my back, while Zane sat beside me with ice on his face. We looked ridiculous.

I opened my book and began reading. Out of the corner of my eye, I saw when Zane rolled his shorts up some, exposing more of his legs to the sun. He'd taken my comment about his pale legs seriously.

"What's so funny?" he asked. Apparently, I hadn't masked my facial expressions very well.

"Oh, something funny in my book." I waved the novel in the air.

"You're a horrible liar. I should probably be glad I picked such a bad liar for a wife."

"Oh, whatever! I'm not a liar!"

"Read me the funny thing in your book." He looked at me and waited.

I looked down at the words I'd been reading. A cheesy college romance wasn't something I wanted to read out loud to Zane. Especially since they'd just kissed. So, I said, "I lost my place." I quickly closed the book before he could snatch it out of my hand and he laughed.

"Brat," he murmured, then added, "Read your book and stop laughing at my legs."

"Sorry," I laughed.

* * *

I STARTED to get hungry and convinced Zane to take me to the restaurant we'd been to the night before. He wore a blue and orange tropical shirt with dark blue shorts, and I chose a matching navy blue sundress with small butterflies of all colors, all over it. I did two French braids down the sides of my head with messy buns at the bottom and put a pair of earrings in. It was the only jewelry I wore since I still didn't have a wedding ring. The only makeup I chose to wear was lip balm. It was hot outside, and knowing me, I'd just sweat it all off since it was only lunchtime.

When I walked out of the restroom, Zane did a double-take, which made me take a second look in the mirror.

"What is it?" I asked.

"Nothing, I just didn't expect you to look so pretty."

My mouth dropped open in horror.

"That came out wrong!" He scrambled across the room and grabbed my hand before I could run to the restroom to change. "You're beautiful all the time; I just wasn't expecting you to look so nice for lunch. I feel like I should change now, that's all I meant."

"Oh," I smiled. "I picked this dress because it matched the outfit you had on."

"Then I won't change."

THE REST of the honeymoon passed in the same fashion. We joked, laughed, and played on the beach like children. Well, I played like a child while Zane smiled at me. We each sported bruises from our twirling incident; Zane's was much worse than mine. Both eyes had blackened, but he was such a good sport about it.

"Men will think you beat me up," he'd said when we went into a little town one night. "They'll know not to mess with you."

I tried to get him to let me put a little makeup on it to cover it up, but he wouldn't let me touch him. He said he'd shave off one of my eyebrows if I got anywhere near him with foundation. I didn't mention it again.

When it was time to leave, I almost cried. I could say I loved being there a hundred times and it wouldn't be enough. I missed my family, but I had lived away from them for almost three years, so I knew I could go a few weeks without seeing them. I had, however, spoken to my parents at the beginning of the trip and they seemed a little more accepting of what happened. They forgave me for keeping it from them, but they weren't happy about who I'd married. Dad tried to scare me with the articles he'd found on the internet, but Zane had already told me what I needed to know and I chose him despite his past.

"I feel safe with you," I said on the night before we left to go home. We'd been lying in bed for only a few minutes, the moon being the only light in the room, when I had the urge to tell him. I felt his eyes on me and rolled over to look at him.

I placed my hand palm up on the space between us, and he glanced at it before looking back into my eyes. He moved his hand on top of mine and intertwined our fingers.

With no more words spoken between us, we fell asleep.

The next morning, Zane surprised me with a question I never saw coming.

"How would you feel if we extended our vacation for another week? There's somewhere in North Carolina I want to take you."

CHAPTER FOURTEEN

Zane

On the last day of our honeymoon, the only thought that kept running through my mind the entire day was that I wasn't ready to go back to real life. Ivy had this incredible gift of making whoever she was around have fun. She had another gift that made the person equally irritated, but I'd known that about her from the moment she got into my car in Ohio.

I'd tried to keep where we were going as much of a secret as I could. We landed in North Carolina and took a cab to Emerald Isle. She'd never been there, or heard of it for that matter.

"I thought Emerald Island was in Florida," she'd said.

"It is. This is Emerald Isle," I answered.

Since it was July, the little island was in full swing. Vacationers that liked a quiet get-away came here to relax in peace. My first time on Emerald Isle had been the year after rehab. Trina recommended I take a break, far away from home and away from people who would make my life miserable. So, I'd come to the island and never wanted to leave. The day before we left Hawaii, I'd called Trina and asked if her brother-in-law would let us rent his house for a week or so, and she called back an hour later telling me he would. She made all the arrangements for Ivy and me with our tickets and had a cab waiting at the airport.

Since we arrived late in the evening, I promised Ivy we would tour the island the next day, so we grabbed dinner and went to Ethan's vacation house.

After we ate, we brought all our bags inside, where she put a load of her clothes into the washing machine. "How did you get this house on such short notice?" Ivy asked.

"It's Trina's brother-in-law's house. He doesn't rent it out since it's his family vacation house. Well, he doesn't rent it out, outside of me."

"I guess you have all the hookups because you're famous?"

She was teasing me, and I turned so she wouldn't see me smile in response.

Over the course of two weeks, Ivy seemed to make me laugh almost every day. I wasn't used to it. I couldn't tell you the last time I'd heard the sound of my laughter. I teetered between being thankful for the distraction and annoyed that she managed to get in my head so quickly.

"Hey, there are two rooms here!" Ivy's voice carried from down the hall, pulling me out of my thoughts. Her comment didn't register until I heard the door of the spare bedroom shut. I made my way down the hall and quickly opened the door.

"Excuse me; I could have been changing or something!"

She placed her hands on her hips and leveled an angry stare at me, apparently awaiting an explanation.

"The bed in this room is too small for the both of us," I said.

"Did you not hear me? There are two bedrooms. Therefore, we can sleep separately."

I reached up to scratch the stubble that covered my chin and cheeks. "I need you to sleep in the bed with me."

"Why?"

"Because I can't protect you if you're in another room."

"Not an acceptable answer," she rolled her eyes and sat on the bed. "Try again."

"Because we're married."

"No one is here. One last shot."

I remained silent, chewing on the inside of my lip, trying my hardest to think of an answer that would be as good as the immediate response I'd said to myself. She wasn't going to move.

"Why do you want me to sleep in the same bed when no one is here to see me?"

"Ivy," I sighed harshly. I felt irritation taking up the forefront of my thoughts, and the fact that I was going to snap and ruin the friendship we'd built scared me. It was either be honest with her or let her sleep in the spare room. I guess if she wanted to sleep there, she would anyway, with or without whatever I planned to say. I sighed again and relented, giving her the explanation even I couldn't understand. "I just sleep better when I know you're beside me. I haven't slept this well in a long time."

Her face relaxed, and she looked like she was going to ask a million questions, so I raised my hand to silence her before she could speak. "I don't want to go into details of my sleeping patterns. That confession was enough soul baring for me for the night, and I'd like to get rest so I can show you the whole island tomorrow. I wanted to bring you here to have fun, and I completely expect you to have a blast."

I turned and walked out of the spare bedroom and into the master. I discarded my shirt and kicked my shoes off into a corner before turning to find Ivy standing in the doorway.

"You can sleep in the other room. I'm not going to force you to do something you don't want to do."

"You forced me to share the master bedroom at home," she said.

"I feel like "forced" is too strong a word for that, and that's different. We have a staff that's there every single day, and Sandro never leaves. I can't take the risk of letting someone find out the truth. I thought you were okay with all of that now."

"I am."

Then why on earth was she bringing it up?

"What are you analyzing?"

She smiled. "How do you know I'm analyzing something?"

I reached into my bag and pulled out a pair of sweats before changing. "Because one side of your mouth pulls down into a frown when you're trying to figure something out. You did it the day I asked you to marry me-."

"You never asked," she interrupted.

"You made the same face when the guy with a pimple officiated our wedding-."

"I was scared the pimple was going to pop!"

"You do it when your dad calls, and when you're trying to

figure out what to get to eat, and when something in your book confuses you. It's your 'thinking face.'"

"For someone that thinks I'm a brat, you sure pay a lot of attention to me."

"I told you on the beach," I took a few steps toward her and stopped. "You're the only person on the face of the planet who I'm concerned with keeping alive, so of course I'll pay attention to every detail."

Her eyes widened with the intensity of my words, even though I'd said them to her before. She took a step back and retreated to the other bedroom. I felt a migraine coming on.

I pulled back the covers and got into bed after turning off the lights, but I was wide awake, scared of what I'd see when I closed my eyes. What nightmare would plague me tonight?

I hadn't lied to Ivy when I told her I'd never slept so well than I did when she was sleeping beside me. She was my dream catcher. I wondered if it was her sweet dreams that kept my dark ones away. Whatever it was, I didn't want it to go away.

Rolling over, I faced the window and stared outside, fighting the urge to fall asleep. I heard the door open, and footsteps cross the room. The covers lifted, and I felt the bed dip slightly. Ivy took a deep breath and sighed, which caused me to smile.

"What made you change your mind?" I quietly asked.

"My feet are cold," she answered.

I rolled over again so I could face her before I grabbed her waist and pulled her toward me. "Put your feet on my legs," I said.

The second her feet touched my legs, I flinched. "How are you this cold?"

"Oh, my goodness, you're a heater!" Ivy closed her eyes and smiled contently.

"You need socks."

"They're in the washing machine, so you'll have to do for tonight."

With her feet resting against my legs, and a smile on both our faces, we drifted off to sleep.

CHAPTER FIFTEEN

Ivy

We were sitting in Zane's office, as we had every night since we'd arrived home from our extended honeymoon the week before. When we got back, Zane kept his promise and took me into Denver to show me around, but other than the nearest grocery store and gas station, I couldn't remember where anything else was. It would be awhile before I had the guts to venture into the city alone.

Zane didn't like to get out of the house very often. Apparently, nothing outside our home was important. His staff didn't even make the list of importance. Sometimes it made me feel awkward, but I think everyone was used to it.

His weird dislike of Sandro was a constant pain, but he seemed to do better if I showed him extra attention when they were both in the same room. It was like having a puppy. I liked puppies, so I guess I couldn't get too upset.

I was reading a few magazine interviews he'd given me, to prepare for our own that was happening in a little over three weeks, while he did whatever it was he did on his laptop.

"We're trending," Zane said from his desk.

"What are you talking about?" I asked.

"The public named us 'Zavy' since Trina released the statement that the marriage was real. We've been trending on social media."

I stood and walked over to look at his computer screen. "Why did they have to choose something that rhymed with gravy? So weird," I said. There were pictures of us I didn't even know people had taken and 'Zavy' was everywhere. The most disturbing articles said that I was pregnant, and another had a picture of Zane's black eyes. That one claimed my father had gotten ahold of him and forced him to marry me.

What in the world is wrong with people? None of these things held a hint of truth.

"I can't wait until we do this interview so people will know the actual story. Well, the real fake story."

"I warned you what was in store."

"I don't think we should look at any more social media, it's poisonous."

Zane looked up at me over his shoulder. "You can't let it affect how you see yourself. I let it tear me up inside when my life fell apart. There are a few reporters out there who tell the truth, but not many. I never wanted my real fans to feel like I didn't appreciate them, but when all I saw was my failure all over the place, I had to get out of the limelight."

"Why do you want to get back into that life so bad?"

"I may have really messed up, but it didn't change the fact that I'd always wanted to act."

"I don't think that's the only reason," I whispered. He tensed, but then took a deep breath and exhaled slowly.

"I don't want the reason I walked away from acting to be because they forced me to. I wanted it to be a decision I made because I didn't want it anymore. At this point, no director trusts me enough to bring me into a project. That's not how I want to go out. I don't want that to be what people remember me by."

I nodded and walked back to the couch to finish reading. "These questions are so personal."

"It comes with the job. I told-,"

"I know," I interrupted. "You told me what to expect. I'm not complaining, I just think it's bizarre that people feel entitled to this information."

"I'm sure you've been obsessed with an actor or two in your life."

"Not like my mom," I smiled. "I had a thing for boy bands when I was younger, but other than that I never watched much television. I explored the woods when I got bored."

"Alone?" he asked.

"Not always. Sometimes one of my siblings would come with me." I put my magazine down so I could see Zane's reaction when I said what I wanted to next. "We should go camping."

It was worth it. He reared his head back like I had hit him, and he looked like someone was trying to force him to swallow a bowl full of worms. I laughed until I couldn't breathe and fell off the couch.

"I don't know if there will ever be another name that will fit you better than 'brat' does."

"I'm sorry. It was just so funny."

"There isn't a force on earth that could get me in a tent in the woods. No, thank you," he said, shaking his head.

"It's not so bad. As long as it's not warm enough for snakes to be crawling around everywhere. Well, there are lots of coyotes around, too. It gets spooky when they all start howling together. Then there's the whole-,"

"Ivy," Zane growled from his desk. "That's enough."

"I was just explaining my experience."

"Well, it's not something you're going to have to worry about ever again."

"Ever?" I asked. Was he crazy?

"I mean, while we're married." He went back to work, completely ignoring me the rest of the evening. He didn't talk to me again until he finished working in his office.

"Let's go eat and go to bed," he said. I'd finished my reading almost an hour before and when I stood to leave he'd asked me to wait for him, so I sat back down and waited.

And waited.

When I asked a question, I he acted as if I hadn't, and then when he was ready, he expected me to be giddy and ready to follow him anywhere? I don't think so!

Jerk.

I waited because I thought he would finish up quickly, but also because I liked thinking he wanted me to be in the room with him. Well, I waited and waited. The hour passed slowly, and I was well into my brooding.

"What's wrong with you?" he asked as I walked past him out of his office. He reached out to grab my arm, but I jerked it out of his grasp. I stormed up the stairs and walked into the kitchen to get a soda.

"Ivy!" he yelled from the basement. I'd left him down there with a questioning look on his face. Finally, he reached the kitchen where I was leaning against the fridge. "What happened?" he asked.

I scoffed. "Are you kidding me? You asked me to wait, and I sat there in silence for an hour. You completely ignored me when I talked to you. That's annoying!"

He smiled, and I narrowed my eyes. "What?" I demanded.

"Ivy, I had headphones in. How was I supposed to know you were talking to me?"

I felt my cheeks heat with the proof of my embarrassment. "Well," I started. "I could have been doing something else the whole time I was waiting for you. You just let me sit there, bored."

"I'm sorry," he was still smiling. " I'm used to you being there while I'm working now. I didn't mean for you to be bored or upset."

"You like working with me in there?" I asked.

"Of course, how else am I going to get through boring emails and calls?"

"I guess that makes it a little better."

"How about you put a bookshelf down there and fill it with books, and later we can get online and you can pick out your own laptop?"

"I don't need my own computer, Zane. I'm fine with what I have, but, a bookshelf would be perfect. Maybe I could set up an easel so I could draw, too."

"You draw?" he asked while he pulled out a frozen skillet meal from the freezer.

"Do I draw? Yes. Is it art? Depends on what you think art is," I laughed. "I can't draw people, but I really like expressionism. Nothing is perfect, that's what makes it great in my opinion. Kelly and Graham are the real artists."

"Siblings?" he asked, and I nodded. He added, "You can get whatever you want. This is your home now, too."

"Can I redecorate the living room so it doesn't look like a single guy with bad taste lives here?"

He chuckled. "I'm telling Rayna you said that. She decorated."

"No, she didn't!" I laughed, and he nodded. "You better not say a word!"

"How are you going to keep me quiet?" he asked. He was pouring the contents of the food into the skillet and looking over his shoulder at me at the same time. What a show off.

"You want hush money?" I feigned shock.

"Hush money, hush kissing. However you want to look at it is up to you."

"You can't be serious."

"Oh, I'm very serious." He turned and crossed his arms over his chest. "Come on, pay up."

"Now?" I asked. I looked around the kitchen for someone to save me, but we were alone.

He smirked. "What's the matter? You've kissed me before."

"Yeah, but never when there wasn't someone watching."

That wasn't the right thing to say. He immediately closed down and turned to stir the food. Although I'd said what I was thinking, I didn't mean it the way it sounded. I walked over to him and put my hand on his arm, pushing back slightly to get him to look at me.

"I didn't mean it the way it must have sounded." I was about to make myself vulnerable to him, but it was something he needed from me. "I want to kiss you, but I guess it scared me because this would be a different kind of kiss. It would be for us and no one else."

"I want," he paused and sighed. "I want a kiss that belongs to just us."

"Me too," I said.

He sat the spoon on the counter and placed his hand on my cheek. "I think you're going to be the death of me," he said before placing his mouth on mine.

The kiss was soft and sweet, only lasting a few short minutes, and when he pulled away, I saw real happiness in his eyes for the first time. It elated me, not only because he seemed to really enjoy our relationship, but because I had caused that happiness.

I wish I had captured that moment and somehow found a way to bottle it up, because hours later when we were both asleep, his phone rang.

I didn't know a phone call could change so much about my life. I didn't even know there was a deeper, darker Zane than I'd already met and grown to care about.

If someone had told me what I was about to go through, I probably would have snuck out the door in the middle of the night, changed my name and ran for the rest of my life.

Too bad that isn't how life works.

CHAPTER SIXTEEN

Ivy

I was standing at the top of the stairs that led down to the basement, shaking, unable to control the jerky movements.

As soon as the phone rang the night before, Zane didn't even get dressed. He ran out of the house in his sweatpants. I wasn't even sure if he put shoes on. I sat in bed, eyes wide and confused, for what seemed like the entire night. I sent him a text message asking if he was okay, but he never responded.

I didn't know when I had fallen asleep, but I woke up to the faint sound of yelling. My heart sped up and as I walked down the stairs, the sound grew louder. When I made it to the basement stairs, I opened the door and stopped. I'd found where the noise was coming from.

I took an unsteady breath before I began the descent down. Finally, reaching the bottom, I spotted Zane in the gym area, furiously pounding on the punching bag. Sweat covered every inch of exposed skin. There were moments he would stop and lean over to breathe, but in those moments, he would begin screaming again. An angry war sound that I'd never heard before. Not from anyone. His voice didn't sound the same. It was cutting in and out, like he was losing his voice, and when he stopped yelling, he would pick right back up, torturing whatever he saw in the punching bag.

I felt a hand wrap around my elbow and I jumped in fear.

"You should come upstairs," the voice whispered. It was Sandro. I looked over my shoulder into the eyes of my bodyguard and wondered how he could be so extremely calm in this situation. Especially when I felt like something inside my body was being physically cut into pieces.

"Come upstairs," he repeated with a little more authority.

I noticed the screaming and punching had stopped so my eyes slowly crawled to where Zane was standing. There were cuts on his eyebrow, cheek and upper lip. I almost gasped aloud, but Sandro's hand tightened on me in warning. Zane was breathing hard. His eyes looked so devoid of everything besides anger and hatred.

For the first time in the weeks since we'd gotten married, I felt afraid of him and what he might do next.

Sandro lightly pulled on my arm, moving me so I stood behind him, then he started walking backwards until my feet hit the stairs.

"Upstairs," he said yet again, but this time, I listened.

When we got to the living room, I stood, looking all around me at the pictures we'd hung on the wall. Zane and I looked happy in all of them, which had been the state of our relationship. I knew whatever had upset Zane wasn't anything I did, but the level of hostility and violence scared me to my core. My body shook as if I was cold, but I knew this was the effect fear had sometimes.

I sought Sandro's eyes. "What was that?"

"Honestly?" He scrubbed his hands over his face in frustration. "I was hoping you knew."

Of course, I should know. I was his wife. "I'll be right back," I said, walking toward the stairs that led upstairs so I could call Trina.

"Hello?" she answered after only a few rings.

"Trina? This is Ivy, Ivy Landis."

"Ivy? Is everything okay?" she asked, something close to fear in her voice.

"No, not really. Uh, it's Zane. I don't know what's going on right now, but he's kind of freaking out in the basement." My voice wavered some, and I felt my eyes fill with tears until I couldn't see past them. I took another unsteady breath and let out what sounded like a whimper. "I don't understand what happened."

"Ivy, listen to me, you aren't in danger, I promise. Please don't leave him."

"What?" I asked, shocked. "Leaving him hadn't been my plan. I'm worried about him!" What in the world was wrong with her? He may have scared me, but I didn't think he'd hurt me.

Trina exhaled harshly. "I know. All you need to do is give him some space for a few days. He'll be back to his old self in no time."

That wasn't what I wanted to hear. I wanted to know what put him in this state to begin with.

"Thanks," I said before hanging up the phone. He may have loved and respected his agent, but I wasn't her biggest fan at the moment. This obviously wasn't the first time he'd done something like this, and maybe it wasn't her secret to tell, but I was feeling a little betrayed on all fronts. I'd been left in the dark by everyone.

I thought about calling my mom, but she would tell my dad and they'd be here before I knew it. I couldn't do that, not to Zane. As his wife, I had to protect him from others and while I loved my family and knew they wouldn't tell a soul; I knew I would be their first concern. So instead, I walked down to the kitchen and started preparing breakfast.

I didn't know what else to do.

Sandro was trailing me everywhere I went. Walking from the fridge to the stove was a task when I had to move around him. I sighed. "What are you doing?"

"I'm here to protect you."

"Yes, I know that, but why are you hovering in my kitchen?"

"Because I don't know what's going on." He sounded on edge and I looked at him.

"Sometimes Zane gets angry. He pounds some sense into his punching bag, and then he's grouchy for a while. It's nothing I can't handle," I lied.

"Why are you crying?"

I lifted my hands to my cheeks and sure enough, there were fresh tears running down them. "I get scared for him," I answered honestly. "I worry about him and that's why I'm crying."

"Does he hit you?"

I reared my head back in shock. "No!" I assured him. "He never has and never will. That's something you shouldn't worry about."

"I don't feel comfortable leaving you alone."

"Then sit down at the island. I think I'll make it around the kitchen in one piece."

He heeded my instruction and sat down.

I was a somewhat decent cook. Not like Zane, but I could manage a breakfast of bacon, eggs and biscuits. I focused all my attention on what I was doing in the kitchen. I refused to think of my husband's bleeding face until I was alone again.

"Are you hungry?" I asked Sandro when I finished. I didn't wait for his answer, giving him a plate filled with food, anyway.

I had two more, and I quickly picked one up and walked to the basement stairs.

"What are you doing?" Sandro called out, hot on my trail.

"I want to take him food," I answered.

"You shouldn't go back down there." I stopped and turned, causing him to stop so he didn't run into me.

"He's my husband, Sandy. I think I can take my husband breakfast." I sounded like a robot to my own ears. Forcing emotion out of one's voice did that.

He didn't move to stop me again, but I felt his presence all the way down the stairs. When I saw Zane sitting on the ground by his bag, I slowly made my way toward him. He glanced up at me and I felt a knife in my heart when I saw the blood. I inhaled through my nose, forcing my mouth to remain shut so I didn't cry out.

I placed the plate beside him on the ground and backed away, like he was a frightened animal. I hated the reference I made in my head. I knew he wasn't an animal, puppy or otherwise, but I didn't have experience in this kind of situation, not with a human anyway. Plenty of times I'd walked up on an animal and had to practice caution. Even the smallest of them would attack if they were scared, I was sure the same was true for people.

I backed into Sandro and he steadied me with his hands

on my arms. Something in Zane's eyes changed when he saw the contact and I quickly stepped out of his grasp, putting a small amount of distance between us.

"I'll be upstairs if you need me," I whispered.

He didn't reply or even acknowledge that I'd spoken. He did, however, pick up his plate and start eating.

I released a relieved breath and turned to go back upstairs.

* * *

ZANE DIDN'T COME to bed that night. Or the night after that. Or the next one.

I lost track of how many hours of sleep I was getting at night. It wouldn't have surprised me if someone told me I wasn't sleeping. Every morning when I went down to check on him, he was pounding his anger into the punching bag. If I could put a name to what I saw, every day it would be wrath.

I tried to text my family rather than call them. I'd found out quickly that nothing was safe in the house while he was in this state. We'd lost two lamps and a picture frame to him throwing it against a wall in the three days since he'd gotten the phone call.

Sandro started sleeping in the spare bedroom across the hall from mine. He said it was because his bed was bad on his back, but I knew he was afraid Zane would come upstairs at night in the state he was in.

The only times Zane had actually walked into the bedroom was to change into different sweats and to shower. He wasn't even shaving anymore.

I called Rayna and told her not to worry about coming

for a while. I assured her she was going to get paid all the same, but I would handle things for a while. I did the same for Zariah. She shocked me when she tried comforting me.

Apparently, they'd witnessed his episodes before.

"What do I do about the bruises?" I asked, fighting tears. It felt like they would never end.

"I know it's hard, but you have to ignore them, Ivy. He's private about everything, and this isn't an exception. He won't talk to anyone about it. I was almost fired when I asked if he was okay the first time I saw it."

"How often does this happen?"

"A few times a year. Just give him a while and he'll be back to normal." She was the second person to tell me that but, it wasn't enough to make me feel better.

I walked to the living room and sat on the couch, looking out the giant window that I hated. I hugged a throw pillow and laid my head on the cushion.

"Maybe you should go stay with your family for a while," Sandro said from beside me.

"I'm not leaving him," I said through clenched teeth. He said the same thing to me every single day.

"I'd go with you too. Did you know that?"

I hesitated before asking, "Why?"

"Because I'm your bodyguard. I'm here to protect you."

"I don't understand why. Nothing is going to happen to me."

"If someone broke in or tried to bother you when you went out, that's where I would come in."

"I never go anywhere."

"If you did," he said. He let the half sentence hang in the air, but I understood what he was saying.

"Can I fire you?"

"No. You didn't hire me, and you don't pay me, so you can't get rid of me."

"That's too bad."

Sandro laughed. It felt wrong, but I didn't say anything.

"Do you know how to play Monopoly?" I asked.

"Yeah," he answered.

"Follow me."

I set up the board game at the island in the kitchen and sat down. I'd found a closet with a few games in it a few days before, and I decided I needed to focus my energy somewhere other than the basement.

* * *

MORE DAYS WENT by and every single morning I felt like my body was going to fall apart. Then I would go downstairs and see Zane's body covered in scratches, fresh blood and old bruises, and I'd feel guilty for feeling any pain at all.

Someone was hurting him almost every other night, and there was nothing I could do. I wanted to call the police, but Sandro talked me out of it. He said if Zane was doing something illegal, I would only get him into trouble. I didn't want that, but I felt helpless.

"You're losing weight." Zane's deep voice made me jump, forcing my heart to pound harder than usual.

I was looking through our closet to find something to wear when he startled me. His voice sounded gruff, cracking like it hurt to speak, and his face held no emotion.

"I'm not eating well," I was honest. I felt a lump grow in my throat. I couldn't believe I was speaking to him. He'd finally said words to me and I wanted to run and throw my arms around him, begging him to never leave me alone like that again. I didn't, though, because his eyes still looked empty.

"You should eat." He was avoiding my eyes, focusing on the ribs I knew were visible underneath my skin.

"Okay," I whispered. He nodded and then walked into the bathroom, locking the door behind him.

I felt like someone had come into the closet and placed weights on my shoulders. I pulled one of his shirts from a hanger, slipping it on, then paired it with the sweats he'd given me on the first night I was there.

Sandro moved into the doorway of the closet and looked at me with a sad smile.

"Go to your family," he said with no conviction.

"I'm not leaving him," I replied, then I walked downstairs and pulled out the Monopoly game.

CHAPTER SEVENTEEN

Ivy

This window was going to be the death of me.

Since I'd figured out Zane's pattern, sleeping when he left to go wherever it was he went proved to be impossible. I'd sit in the living room and wait for him to come home the next morning. If he noticed me, he said nothing, but I knew that he knew my whereabouts. Even with whatever he had going on, I didn't see him giving up control. Zane always had knowledge of all his surroundings.

I never thought I'd say it, but watching the sunrise now grated on my nerves.

The sun had just come up behind the houses across the street when a maroon car I'd never seen pulled into the driveway. My heart stopped, wondering if someone was coming to tell me my husband had died in the night.

"Sandro!" I yelled as I rushed to the door. I must have scared him while he took a drink of his coffee because the sound of glass shattering filled the house. "Sorry!"

I flung the door open and was greeted by a young man with his fist raised, about to knock. He looked shocked and confused for a moment before recognition hit him.

The same couldn't be said for me, though. I didn't recognize him at all. He stood well over a head taller than me, and his dark brown eyes made him seem friendly. His shaggy light brown hair was long enough to hang over his ears, and his smile gave him a boyish charm. He looked too happy to be delivering bad news.

"You must be Ivy," he smiled and stuck out his hand. "My name is Thomas Fields, but you can call me Tommy. I'm an old friend of Zane's and I've been meaning to stop by for quite some time now. I figured today was the day."

I looked over my shoulder at Sandro and gave him a questioning look. He looked right back at me like I was an idiot.

Right. I was the wife, I should know this stuff.

"Would you like to come in for some coffee?" I asked, ignoring the warning in my stomach. Sandro was here if I needed him or the gun his shirt covered.

Tommy grinned. "Absolutely, thank you!"

I moved, allowing him to come inside, and I walked to the kitchen. Sandro composed his expression, but I could feel the judgment coming off him. He didn't realize it, but he knew just about as much about Zane as I did, and we both knew he wouldn't like me letting a man into the house.

"I heard about Zane getting married, even saw a few pictures of you two on your honeymoon in a magazine."

"Yeah, I wasn't even aware some of them were being taken at the time," I admitted. "It's the weirdest thing to me."

"So, you aren't famous or anything?" he asked. He pulled

out a chair at the island and sat down, making himself at home. Maybe he'd been here before.

"That depends on who you ask. I was super famous back home because I burned off our gym teacher's eyebrows, but in the real world, I'm a nobody."

"Not anymore." I handed Tommy a cup filled with coffee and smiled.

"I guess you're right." Sandro caught my eye with a wave. I looked at him and waited for something, but he just stared at me. Weirdo. "So, I don't mean to be rude, but is there a reason for your visit?"

"Honestly, not really. I haven't heard from Zane in a few years and heard he lived around here. I visited his mom, and she told me where I could find his place."

So he hadn't been here before.

"He's usually back by now, but I guess something must have held him up. I'm sure he'll be here any minute, but I can call him if you'd like."

"Hey, why would I want to look at his ugly mug when I could talk to a pretty girl instead?" I saw Sandro roll his eyes.

"You know what's crazy?" he asked. I shook my head. "I've been friends with Zane since we were eighteen years old, and I would never have pegged him for the type to get married."

I took a sip of coffee and shrugged. "People change. I'm confident that Zane isn't the same person he was back then."

"He told you about all that?"

"You seem surprised."

"I guess I shouldn't be since anyone could find the info on the internet, anyway."

"Where did you meet Zane?" I asked.

He moved his hand through his hair and chuckled. "That's probably not a story you want to hear."

"Okay?" An awkward silence followed until I couldn't stand it anymore. "Do you know how to play Monopoly?"

"Of course I do! Who doesn't?"

"Sandro, will you go get the game out of the closet?"

"Uh, no, but you can."

"Oh, right! You can't leave me alone with the stranger with pretty hair." I said before I headed toward the hall closet. I heard Tommy laugh and couldn't help but smile too. Something was off about our visitor, but apparently I was craving human interaction so badly I was willing to ignore it.

Maybe I'd fix something to eat and be able to get some food in my stomach today.

"I'm the shoe. I'm always the shoe," I said as I walked back into the kitchen.

"Fine by me!" Tommy rubbed his hands together like he was warming up. "I just want to warn you, I'm really good at this game."

"You can't be good at a game of chance," Sandro huffed from where he still stood.

"Ignore him. He's just cranky because I won the last three games we played."

"Come play a game with us, man," Tommy offered him the wheelbarrow and waited. Sandro's eyes moved from the game piece to Tommy to me before he finally gave in and took the peace offering.

"Before we get started, do you mind if I use the restroom?" Tommy asked.

"It's around the corner," I said, pointing him in the right direction.

When we heard the restroom door shut and lock, Sandro was in my face.

"I can't give you a solid reason, but I don't like him. I have a bad feeling and I just know as soon as Zane gets home, someone is going to die."

"Obviously Zane isn't coming home, so shut up!" I whispered. "I don't have warm fuzzy feelings about the guy, but maybe I can find out what Zane's been up to."

"How are you still alive when you're this stupid? You let a man in your house that you don't even know!"

"Yeah, so did my mom and look how that ended for her; she married the guy and had thirty kids! Listen, all I want is to figure out what my husband has been doing. I can't live like-." The front door opened, effectively cutting me off mid-sentence. My eyes widened in fear and Sandro looked almost sad.

"Whatever happens, this is on you," he whispered.

I turned in time to see Zane step into the archway of the kitchen. My breath hitched as I took in how bad he looked.

"Whose car?" he asked. His voice cracked in and out painfully, making it clear he was in a lot of pain.

"Zane," I raised my hands, trying to calm him, but it was too late.

"I hope you're ready to get your butts kicked in this game!" Tommy hollered from the hallway.

Zane knew who it was. I didn't need his words because his entire body reacted. His eyes darted to mine, and he looked like I'd betrayed him with every fiber of my being.

Before Tommy even made it to the kitchen, he was down on the ground. Zane had his hands wrapped around Tommy's neck, but the guy didn't even look scared. He smiled like this was the normal life for him and it sent a chill up my spine.

"Sandro, get your gun out," Zane growled.

"Already have it, boss." I wrenched my head around and stopped cold when I saw the gun in Sandro's hand. He had it aimed at Tommy and Zane.

What was going on?

Zane was talking to Tommy low enough so that I couldn't hear him. I tried to step closer, but Sandro grabbed my arm, not letting me move forward.

"Sandro?" Zane's voice was thick with anger.

"I've got 'em."

Zane finally released Tommy's throat and allowed him to stand. Before he left, he stopped and smiled at me.

"It was nice meeting you, Beautiful," he said, right before Zane punched him in the jaw. I screamed and covered my face with my hands, already trying to get the image out of my head.

What in the world was happening?

The front door shut, and I heard the locks slide into place before I felt a hand on my wrist. I moved my hands away from my eyes and looked up at Sandro. I was about to break down and cry when I saw movement out of the corner of my eye. I turned to see Zane staring daggers.

"Come here," he said roughly. I shook my head no and took a step back. "Sandro, leave us alone."

"Boss, maybe you want to go cool off first."

"Go!" he shouted.

Sandro looked down at me and gave me a sad smile. "I'll be in the living room."

When Zane and I were finally alone, I tried to absorb all that had happened. I was still worried about him, but I was afraid of him too. I had no idea what he was going to do or say.

"Did your parents teach you nothing?" he spat. "I've met idiots, but this has to be the dumbest thing I've ever witnessed someone do."

Ouch. That hurt. "I'm not an idiot," I said pitifully.

"No? Ivy, you just let a drug dealer into our house! And not just any drug dealer, but the one that helped me right down Addiction Boulevard. He's why I was in rehab! He obviously didn't care that you're married, so what do you think would have happened had Sandro not been here?"

"How was I supposed to know who he was? I wouldn't have had to answer the door if you were here, so how is this on me? All he said was that he was an old friend!"

"What kind of old friends do you think I have?" he yelled. "I wasn't a good person!" He pinched the bridge of his nose and winced. "I can't deal with this right now. From now on, you're not allowed to answer the door for anyone. Do you understand?"

When I nodded, he stormed out of the kitchen and went upstairs. A few moments later, I heard the water turn on.

I lowered myself to the floor. Every muscle in my body was tight, and my eyes stung. Without my permission, days of pent up frustration and worry burst through in the loudest sob I'd ever released. I cried, and I cried hard. I couldn't breathe. I couldn't think. All I knew was that my heart was in so much pain.

When I'd let out every tear, Sandro stepped back into the kitchen.

"Go home," he said.

I took a deep breath. "I am home," I replied.

I made my way upstairs to our bedroom and sat on the

floor, waiting for Zane to get out of the shower. After a few minutes, the water turned off, and he opened the door. He stopped to stare at me for a second before he walked into the closet to get dressed. I heard him grunt in pain.

I stepped into the doorway to see him struggling to get a t-shirt on. "Do you need help?" I asked.

He didn't answer me, so I walked to his shirts and pulled one down that had the sleeves cut out. It was ripped up and didn't really cover much, but I knew he used them to work out in.

"You'll have to wear this one if you can't get a regular shirt on. Maybe we should call a doctor, just to make sure you didn't crack a rib or something." I approached Zane slowly and waited for him to stop struggling with his clothes.

He sighed, dropped the shirt onto the floor and sat on the stool he used when he put his shoes on. I moved closer and pushed the muscle shirt up his arms before stretching it enough to get it over his head.

"I don't understand why you're still here," he grunted. "Haven't I scared you off by now?"

"What? You thought a little blood and brooding was going to make me run away?" I forced a laugh. He had no idea how close I'd been to running. "You forget, I grew up in Ohio with a bunch of brothers. If you're trying to get rid of me, you'll have to try a little harder than that."

As soon as I said the words aloud, I couldn't help but silently beg him not to try harder. I wasn't sure how much more I could take. I really didn't think what I was going through was worth the deal I'd made with Zane, but he was my friend and I couldn't abandon him when he so obviously needed someone. Just thinking about leaving so I didn't have to worry made me feel incredibly selfish.

He reached up and ran a finger under my eye. It was obvious that I'd been crying.

"Are you sleeping in here tonight?" I asked.

"No," he answered immediately, dropping his hand. He hadn't slept in our room through this entire ordeal, so I don't know why it hurt so bad that he'd shut it down so quickly. I guess I'd hoped since he let me help him, he'd want us to get back to normal.

I was so wrong.

The minute he stood, his face closed off, shutting me out completely.

I'd been in bed for nearly an hour when the urge to go down to the basement was too much to bear. I crept past Sandro's temporary bedroom and scurried down to the first floor as quietly as I could. I knew if the bodyguard woke up, I would be done for. I rolled my eyes. The man acted as if I were a child.

When I got to the basement door, I cracked it open slightly and listened. I didn't hear anything, so I made my way down into the basement.

The only light in the entire room was coming from the television. A quick glance at Zane confirmed my suspicion that he'd fallen asleep because there was no way he'd intentionally watch a cheesy romance.

I picked up the large blanket he kept on the recliner and, trying not to wake him, I covered him up. After turning on the lamp, I picked up a novel and sat on the recliner to read. I fell asleep soon after the heroine in my story decided to stay with the hero instead of traveling to Alaska to find herself a husband.

When I woke up, the lamp was turned off and Zane was gone. I shifted to get more comfortable and noticed the large blanket was now thrown over me. Before I could help myself, I pulled the corner toward my nose and inhaled the scent of my husband.

I sighed.

How could I possibly miss his smell?

CHAPTER EIGHTEEN

Ivy

We were less than three hours away from our interview for the magazine company Trina set up for us, which put me at over three weeks of no sleep.

While I'd listened to Zane when he told me to start eating, and you could no longer see my ribs, I still felt like I'd been beaten down.

Zane, on the other hand, looked like he'd been beaten up, because he had been. His eyes were black, and he had one large cut currently healing on his forehead. His beard, that hadn't been touched in nearly a month, covered whatever wounds he had on or around his mouth. It was under his shirt that looked the worst. Bruises of all colors covered his ribs and back.

When he'd come upstairs that morning to remind me of the interview, I almost cried and pleaded for him to reschedule. I wasn't strong enough to look like nothing was wrong, especially in front of someone that would ask us such personal questions. I tried to control my shaking fingers as he went through the things I was and wasn't allowed to talk about. The last few weeks were on the 'not' list.

I was allowed to gush about our honeymoon and how happy I was, making things up if I needed to. He told me I wasn't allowed to answer anything personal about him, but could answer whatever questions I wanted about my life before I met him.

He told me I could make up our love story.

I stood, straightening my yellow, knee-length dress, when I heard the doorbell ring. I walked into the hall to see Sandro standing, waiting for me. He gave me a reassuring smile and followed me to the door since this was the only way I was now allowed to answer it. Allowing a drug dealer into your home apparently makes your husband lose trust in your judgement.

We all knew it was the people from the magazine, but Zane and Sandro didn't like to take chances.

I opened it to a woman the same height as me. She was dressed in a suit, looking business-like all the way down to her very adorable glasses. I gave her a reserved smile and stretched out my hand to shake hers.

"Hello, you must be Laurel, I'm Ivy."

"Hello, Mrs. Landis. Nice to meet you." She looked like she was struggling between excitement and trying to remain professional.

"Please, follow me," I said, leading her into the living room. "Would you like a cup of coffee? Water?"

"No, thank you. I'm okay."

"If you'll have a seat, I'll go tell Zane you're here."

She smiled, and I left the room in search of Zane. He was where I thought he'd be, in the basement, shut inside his office. Without knocking I opened the door. The laptop was closed, and he was resting his head on his arms that were folded on his desk.

"Zane," I spoke into the silence. "She's here."

He lifted his head and looked at me for a moment before he stood. When he reached me, for some stupid reason, I thought he would hug or reassure me somehow. All he said was, "Don't mess up," and he left. I forced the hurt away and told myself it didn't matter. It wasn't like we were in love, and we didn't have a real marriage by any means. I told myself that I couldn't care less about his words or his attitude toward me. My thoughts were ineffective, though. I cared about him too much to not care about how he'd been treating me.

Instead of being the beaten down, depressed girl I felt like, I squared my shoulders and pulled out the attitude I'd been graced with at birth. I walked into the living room and sat beside Zane on the couch. Laurel was seated on the chair and Sandro was standing in the corner of the room, quirking an eyebrow at me. I gave him a confident smile and grabbed Zane's hand in my own.

"My name is Laurel," she said to my husband. He only nodded.

"Okay." She hesitated to turn her phone recorder on. "So, I wanted to thank you both for sitting down with me today. This is going to be our Christmas Special, so I'm really excited to get through the interview and start pictures! We have a tree and everything."

"Wow," I said with a smile. "That sounds like it's going to be messy, but fun."

"First thing's first!" She grinned. "Congratulations on your marriage!"

I let out a girly giggle. "Thank you!"

"The public was in for quite a shock when pictures started surfacing, and there were rumors about a secret marriage! Why did you decide to keep it so hush-hush?"

"Well," I started. I looked at Zane and saw his eyes on me. It didn't matter what had gone on in the last couple of weeks. His intense stare made me blush. "Uh, what was the question?" I asked.

She laughed. "I can see the honeymoon phase is far from over. A simple look from him and you turn as red as a tomato."

His look was far from simple.

I leaned close to Zane and placed a kiss over his bearded cheek. "I can't help it."

Finally, I felt a difference in not only the room but in Zane as well. His body seemed to lessen its strain, so he no longer felt like a spring under pressure. He leaned back and moved his arm so he was holding me to his side. He moved his face to the crook of my neck and took a deep breath. I barely heard the, "I'm sorry," he whispered in my ear before he pulled his face away and looked back at Laurel.

"We kept it quiet because I didn't feel like it should be anyone's business when I was getting married. I wanted to have a moment of peace with my wife, before everyone bombarded us." His voice was hoarse from the rough treatment he'd given it, but he was still just as fierce.

I ducked my head to try to hide my smile. I didn't care if that particular comment was for the public, he'd apologized and seemed to relax beside me. My heart thundered in my chest as I sat there, listening to him answer a few questions about his family's reaction.

"How about your family, Ivy? Were they just as shocked as Zane's?" she asked.

"I'd say they were a little more than shocked." I forced out a laugh. "My parents were really upset that I hadn't told them what was going on, but it all happened so fast!"

Laurel asked us quite a few more questions and let us know a camera crew would be coming by to take pictures of us a few hours later. I hadn't known there would be a photoshoot, but Zane assured me there would be people bringing me plenty of clothes. That only made it feel even more weird.

I wasn't aware of how much time and effort it took to publish only a few photos. I felt incredibly sorry for all the crew, so I called Rayna and begged her to come cook a huge meal for everyone. I think Zane wanted to kill me after that because I made everyone sit down to eat and, since his island only sat two people, most were sitting in the living room on the couch and floor.

I noticed one of the younger guys watching Zane from a distance and wasn't surprised when he finally approached him. After finding out it was one of the photographer's sons, I sat back and observed their interaction. Zane seemed to be surprised by the attention. Even though it was my first, and hopefully only photoshoot, I thought it was pretty basic knowledge that all parties involved were going to be looking at you. I laughed every time Zane would turn around and find the boy close behind. He finally looked up and searched me out in the room. His eyes narrowed when I smiled widely.

Without a sound, his lips formed the words I could clearly read as, "Come here." He beckoned me with his hand.

I was saved by Kimber, the leader of the whole production, asking everyone to get back to work. It was well after midnight when the crew had everything packed up and ready to leave.

* * *

"I THINK that boy really liked you." I said, breaking the silence later that night in bed. I knew he wasn't asleep yet by his breathing and decided if we were awake, I might as well talk to him.

"Yeah, and I think you're a little brat for leaving me to talk to him alone," he answered. The lights were off, but I knew he was lying on his side, facing me.

"What was I supposed to do?" I laughed.

"You were supposed to come over and say you needed to talk to me or something. Not leave me in an awkward situation with a kid that thinks I'm, 'The coolest guy I ever saw, dude.'" I felt the bed shake with his silent laughter and couldn't help the one that burst from my own mouth.

"I didn't know he said that."

"Well, he did." I smiled and closed my eyes, replaying the day. I'd never had so much fun with something so weird. Maybe weird wasn't the right word, but it was certainly very different to me. I came from an average sized town in Northern Ohio, where the majority of people knew each other. Living there had made me feel as if I'd been trapped in a box. This? This was completely different from my life, even my life in Taylorsville.

Zane hadn't taken me anywhere besides Hawaii and North Carolina, which was still the greatest time of my life, but even being at home with him felt different.

"What are you thinking about?" Zane asked.

"What would you think about going to visit my family for a while?" I was overcome with nostalgia, thinking about my hometown and how much I missed the Murphy crew.

"How long is a while?" he asked after a moment.

"Maybe a week?" I paused before I added, "I miss my family."

I felt him shift on the bed and his hand found my cheek and slowly ran his fingers over my hair. I shifted and pulled his other arm under my head, so I was using him as a pillow.

He must have felt the tear hit his bicep because he moved even closer and whispered, "Please don't cry, baby."

"I'm sorry."

"Why are you crying?" he asked.

"I've just been so worried about you. I didn't know what to do." He stiffened, then relaxed when he realized I wasn't going to say more.

"You were exactly the way I needed you to be, if that helps at all."

"I think Sandro thought you were going to hurt me if I got too close."

"Ivy, I would never, ever hurt you. I would die before I laid a finger on you. Plus," he added with humor lacing his words, "You've made it perfectly clear that you'll cut me."

"I will," I said, sniffling. "Are you going to tell me what happened, or will you at least tell me who Tommy is to you and why he showed up here?"

Zane was silent for a long time and I was almost convinced he'd fallen asleep when he finally whispered, "Tommy is nothing to me and he'll never show his face here again, that I can promise you. Let's go see your family for a week. We can leave Thursday, if you want."

He didn't say anything else, and I tried to not to let it hurt that he wouldn't trust me with whatever he'd gone through. Maybe one day he would rely on me and I hoped it was sooner rather than later, but then again, I hoped he never had to live through that again.

CHAPTER NINETEEN

Zane

We bought plane tickets to Ohio the next morning and left a couple days after that. I did everything I could to make sure I left my demons at home because I knew how much this trip meant to Ivy. I didn't want to fail her anymore than I already had.

When she'd kissed me during the interview, it was as if that simple act leached the darkness that clouded my mind. If only it could stay that way, forever.

According to Ivy, we were only minutes away from the home she grew up in. She was literally bouncing in her seat like it was Christmas morning. Her joy was infectious. But every time I smiled, I remembered Sandro was in the car as well, driving.

She'd insisted that he come with us so he wouldn't be alone and bored at home, and when we arrived to pick up the car we rented, she asked him to drive.

Whatever.

I closed my eyes and breathed through my nose. I didn't completely understand this need to be her everything all of a sudden. Every time she wanted Sandro to do something with or for her, I wanted to fire him. It was insane. I told myself it was because I didn't want Ivy to fall for Sandro and make my life even worse in the media, but that wasn't true at all. I owed him a great deal of thanks for taking such good care of my wife while I wrestled with-.

"There it is!" Ivy squealed, invading my thoughts.

I looked up to see a large two story home in the middle of a clearing, surrounded by trees. There were horses, goats, and a cow in the fence on one side of the driveway and about twelve cars on the other side. Apparently they were having a family reunion.

"Who are all these people?" I asked.

"They're my family!"

You've got to be kidding. "You are blood related to every single person in that house?"

"Blood doesn't make you family, Zane," she answered. "But yes, they are all my family."

We parked, and it was like magic. As soon as Sandro cut the engine, the door to the house flew open and about ten thousand people ran outside like they were fleeing zombies.

Ivy started screaming and trying to take off her seatbelt, but she was too excited to focus on one task. I reached over and undid her seatbelt and she jumped out of the car, running into the first person's set of arms. She was about the same size as Ivy, but her hair was much longer and she looked older. I assumed it was her mother, but there were so many people, I couldn't be sure.

She filed through everyone and I didn't know whether to relax or be afraid when I recognized a few faces. Her Aunt

Sam, her grandfather and the cousin that called her were all in the crowd. Her cousin came up to me first, as well as he could on crutches.

"Hey, new cuz," he said, grabbing me in an awkward over the crutches hug. I patted his back.

"Don't kill me, but I forget your name," I said.

"No problem. I'm Callahan, but you can call me Cal. This is my brother, Logan." He pointed to the guy walking up beside him. Logan had long hair pulled back into a ponytail and tattoos from his hands to his neck. I knew that for sure because his shirt was off. He had piercings in his face and ears, too. I shook his hand and said, "Nice to meet you, Logan."

"You, too." His smile was genuine.

"You must be Zane." A deep voice said to my left, and I turned to face a man about my height. "I'm Phil, Ivy's grandfather."

I didn't miss the narrowing of his eyes or the clenched fists at his side. If he was her grandpa, then he definitely was nearing seventy years old, but there wasn't a doubt in my mind he would be able to take me down. He was built differently than the other grandpa I'd met when I had my car worked on, but he looked no less strong.

"It's nice to meet you, Phil." I stretched out my hand, praying he'd see it as a peace offering and forgive me for marrying Ivy before letting her tell her family. When he took my hand and slowly smiled, I felt a weight lift off my shoulders. If I had her grandpa's forgiveness, surely I'd have her dad's, too.

"Zane," Ivy yelled. She was standing with the woman she'd hugged as soon as we got there, and a man that was almost a foot taller than both of them. I knew in my gut I was about to meet her mom and dad, and if the look on her dad's face was any indication on how this would go, it wasn't going to be as easy as I'd hoped.

"Zane, this is my mom and dad, Bentley and Brennan." I smiled tightly and her mom immediately hugged me. It was unexpected, but I returned the embrace, then grabbed Ivy's hand when her mom stepped away. Ivy moved closer to me, wrapping her arm around my lower back and smiled at her parents. "Guys, this is my husband, Zane."

"Nice to meet you, Zane," her mom said. "We were so excited when Ivy told us you'd both be coming for a week." Her dad made a noise that sounded like an objection, but it was met with her mom elbowing him in the stomach.

"Ivy's missed you all so much." I glanced down at her and smiled. "Anytime you want to come and see our home, feel free. Let me know and I'll pay for your plane tickets."

"We can buy our own tickets," her father spat. It was strange, the way he was looking at me. It brought back memories of when I first started acting and how some older cast would look at me like I was stupid. Foolish, even. His attention made me feel small, but I promised myself I would make this trip great for Ivy. Her opinion was the only one that mattered to me.

"Dad, please be nice," Ivy whispered just loud enough for him to hear. She looked around at the family scattered around the yard and looked back at him. "I don't want you making a huge scene in front of everyone."

He took a deep breath and looked into my eyes. "I'm not okay with what happened. I'm not okay with you whisking my daughter away in the middle of the night when no one even knew who you were. All I know about you is what I can find on the internet and I know I can't believe everything I read, so I'm offering you one chance. If you hurt my kid in any way, shape or form, nothing is going to stop me from doing what parents do best. Protecting what's ours, no matter what it takes."

Ivy's arm tightened around me, and I drew encouragement from it.

"Thank you for the chance. It's more than I'd be willing to offer if it were my daughter," I said, honestly. He nodded and then hugged Ivy when she threw herself at him.

She turned and grinned at me. "Are you ready to meet everyone?"

I looked around and laughed, "I guess as ready as I'll ever be. There's no way I'm remembering all these names, though."

"Don't worry, I'll help you learn them all," she said. She grabbed my hand and pulled me toward her aunt that I'd already met. "This is my Aunt Sam and Uncle Ryan. They live in Taylorsville, of course, near my Grandpa Isaac and Grandma Maria," She gestured to the older couple standing beside her aunt and uncle then she moved on. I glanced over my shoulder to see them laugh and shake their heads at her.

"This is my oldest brother, Jake. He's in school for criminal justice right now because he wants to be a cop." She hugged him and didn't give him a chance to say anything before we were moving on. He shook his head and laughed.

Again, and again, she would introduce me to someone then walk away as if we were on a time crunch and didn't have a moment to waste on polite greetings. I laughed a few times but let her drag me behind her.

"This is my sister, Kelly." She stopped at a young girl with pretty long red hair, green eyes and freckles. She looked to be a few years younger than Ivy. "How are you feeling?" Ivy asked her.

Kelly's cheeks reddened immediately, and she looked at me like I knew what was going on. "I'm fine, Ivy!" The young girl hissed.

"Okay, I was just asking," Ivy said before dragging me away, yet again. I met her brothers Parker, Graham and Duke, and finally met Rosa when we went in the house.

I'd known she had a few siblings, but meeting the family in person was an unforgettable experience.

Ivy's mom and dad made a huge dinner for everyone and once we sat down in the back yard where there were a few picnic tables, the questions started coming. They asked about how we met and how I convinced Ivy to marry me. Graham, the brother that was decked out head to toe in black, said he was surprised Ivy married anyone at all since she was so obsessed with traveling the world. I didn't disagree because from the moment I met her; it was what she'd talked about.

I was asked questions about being an actor and finally, the youngest kid, Duke, brought up the subject I'd hoped everyone would avoid.

"Have you really done drugs?" he asked, mouth full of burger. Everyone around us immediately stopped talking and even though we were in the wide open outside, it was as if a bubble holding in the surrounding tension. I didn't like talking about things from my past. There are just some doors that you never open once they're closed. It took a lot for me to be able to tell Ivy, but it was in my best interest to do so. Trina was really the only person that could openly talk about it with me because she'd worked so hard to help me out of it.

"Duke!" I directed my gaze to their mom, who was looking at him with obvious disappointment. I expected people to look shocked or even curious, but the more I looked around me, the more I realized no one was actually looking at me. They were all looking at the kid. "You know better than to ask people those types of questions."

"I was just curious!" he argued. I thought they would expect me to answer since the question was already out there, but I was surprised again when their dad cut in and told him to finish dinner and go to his room. I felt guilty that I hadn't spoken up on his behalf, but when Ivy and I were finally alone, she explained it to me.

"My parents were strict in a very strange way when I was growing up," she laughed. "We weren't allowed to judge people."

"How could your parents be strict about your opinions?" I asked, confused.

"It wasn't about them not respecting our opinion, it was more about teaching us how to shape an opinion. Circumstances don't make a person who they are, it's how they get through them that makes them."

"So, I guess by their standards I'm not a great person since I reacted to my circumstance in a bad way?"

"Not at all. At first my dad was really scared because the last he'd heard was when you were in a bad place a few years back, but once I told him about you, he relaxed and could allow himself to be angry at what you'd done."

"And what was that?"

"You stole his daughter," she laughed again. I surprised myself with a laugh of my own.

"Well, if I could go back and change it," I stopped and really thought about what I wanted to say. Ivy's smile slipped, obviously afraid of what I was going to say. I decided on the truth. "I wouldn't."

She ducked her head and smiled at her shoes. Lucky shoes.

* * *

HOW THE WEEK went by so quickly, I didn't know. One minute I was playing video games with Jake, the next, walking through the woods with Ivy and then before I knew it, Sandro was sitting at the steering wheel, driving us toward the airport.

"I think my little sister has a crush on you," Ivy said to Sandro. He looked in the rearview mirror and smiled at her.

"I was scared your dad was going to kill me just for fun if she tried to sit by me again."

"Rosa's a big flirt. She's only thirteen and I can't even begin to imagine what kind of trouble she's going to get into as she gets older."

"Didn't I overhear your mom telling a story about you stealing Christmas lights from the drama department and decorating your high school with them?" I asked, already laughing.

"It's not funny!" She tried to keep a straight face and failed. "I couldn't say no to a dare."

"Who dared you to do it?" Sandro chuckled.

"Pop did, if you can believe it!" Her laughter filled the car, and I watched as a tear rolled down her face. Holding her belly, she tried to sober up to finish her story. "I've never told anyone that." She paused again, trying to catch her breath. "I wanted to join the drama club, but they said I couldn't because I wouldn't take it seriously."

"Would you have?" I asked.

"Probably not." She sighed, still smiling widely. "I think I would have gotten kicked out pretty quickly."

I sat and listened to her and Sandro exchange stories from when they were kids after that, trying hard to ignore the fire that she'd ignited in my chest.

CHAPTER TWENTY

Ivy

"You're fired!" I picked up an egg and threw it at Sandro, who was trying to flee the kitchen. "Get back here, you coward! Face me like a real man!"

His deep laugh met my ears, and I wiped the raw egg yolk off my face. I'd been minding my business, making breakfast, when Sandro walked into the kitchen, glanced over my shoulder and grabbed an egg. I didn't know he'd intended to smash it on my head, because if I did I would have smacked him with the spatula before it happened.

I grabbed another egg and walked toward the basement stairs, where I knew he had run. I made my way down the steps and carefully looked around the open room, trying to pick out anything that looked out of place. I barely saw movement in a chair that was facing the opposite direction and smirked. What an idiot.

I quietly made my way across the room and ducked

behind him so I could remain unseen. After a silent deep breath, I stood and quickly smashed the egg on his head.

"That'll teach you to mess with me!" I laughed, but it died in my throat quickly. He stood and turned, facing me as the egg slowly slid through his blonde hair and into his face. His eyes narrowed, and I took a step back, but he stalked me as if I were his prey.

"Zane?" I asked, my voice on the edge of panic. He didn't answer, although his eyes darted to the egg that was still visible on my head.

Out of nowhere, he rushed at me and grabbed my middle, lifting and bouncing me over his shoulder. I let out a scream as his arms wrapped around my legs and he ran up the basement stairs. I closed my eyes, thinking if I didn't watch us fall to our deaths then it wouldn't hurt as bad. He reached the top, and I opened my eyes in time to see Sandro standing in the basement grinning like a madman.

"Zane," I screamed. "What are you doing?"

He still didn't give me an answer, but before I knew it, he was opening the back door and running into the backyard. His plan registered in my brain a full three seconds before I felt his jump and we were submerged in the warm water of the swimming pool. He released my legs, and I swam to the surface of the water. He was already there, smiling at me like he'd won.

"My cell phone was in my pocket," I said, glaring. His answering laugh was deep, and he shrugged his shoulders.

"I'll get you a new one." He swam closer, and I tried to retreat, but my back hit the edge. He closed the distance and placed both hands on either side of my head, holding onto the side of the pool. My hands automatically went to his shoulders to stop his advance or hold myself up, I wasn't sure.

"Why'd you smash an egg on my head?" he asked. I could feel his breath on my face and couldn't help but be distracted by how his hair had grown out and laid flat on his forehead from the water. He looked so boyish and playful, and I wished I could see his dimples that were hidden under his two-week-old beard.

"I thought you were Sandro," I answered, barely above a whisper. He glanced at my lips and back to my eyes.

"Why were you chasing Sandro around the house?" His voice lowered, and I felt the hairs on the back of my neck stand.

"Because he smashed an egg on my head while I was cooking."

"What did you do about it?"

"I fired him," I answered. Humor flashed in his eyes, but he covered it up and I swallowed down my nerves.

"You got egg on my favorite chair," he whispered. He paused before asking, "Was it worth it?"

I couldn't answer, so I shook my head no, hoping it would be enough. His eyes darted to my lips again, and this time they stayed.

"Are you going to kiss me?" I asked. His eyes slowly crawled up my face to meet my own.

"Do you want me to?"

I'd barely whispered my, "Yes," when he slammed his mouth against mine. My hands went from his shoulders to his face and I pulled him closer. I felt the burn that told me I was about to cry, but tried to ignore it as I poured my feelings into that moment. I pictured the first night he'd come home, from wherever he was, with a cut up and bleeding face, and how I never, ever wanted to see that again. I remembered walking out of my parents' home and seeing him sitting on the porch with my dad, just talking, and how full my heart felt.

He pulled away, and it felt like he was staring into my soul. I was scared he would be able to see my emotions that were on the surface, so I looked down at his chest. His left hand moved, and I saw a glint of white gold from his wedding band before he placed his hand under my chin, gently lifting my face to look at him.

"Let's go inside and get some dry clothes on. I can make you something to eat if your eggs are burnt."

"Zane?" I stopped him from moving away. "Why haven't you gotten any invitations yet?"

The painful look in his eye told me he knew what I was talking about. It had been bothering me for weeks now. The whole purpose of our marriage was to make it look like he'd settled down and left his party days behind. He had left them behind, but the public wouldn't believe his word. I knew that.

He gave me a sad smile and said, "Things like this just take time, Ivy. It'll happen eventually."

"Maybe we should go out more and let people see you." I suggested. Even though I married him to help him, it was different now. I wanted him to achieve his dreams because he was my friend. I cared about his success.

"Yeah, maybe. It's hard to catch the camera's eye when we're in Denver, Colorado, though," he chuckled.

"Well," I grinned, "That just means that you're going to have to take me to see the world so that the world can see you. It's a win-win."

"Of course that would be your answer," he teased, kissing

my forehead. "Maybe you're right. I should get back out there."

"Are you scared? Is that what's been stopping you?"

"Yes and no," he admitted. He looked embarrassed but continued. "Of course I'm always going to be leery about being in the public because of how everyone turned their backs on me so quickly, but, honestly, I've been pretty content lately."

"What do you mean?"

"I guess I didn't realize how much having a friend would change what I thought was important."

"What's important to you now?" I asked, allowing myself to smile.

"You're important to me, now. I want to make sure you're safe all the time, but even more than that, I want to make sure you're happy. I don't want you to regret this time we have together."

"I am happy." I confessed as if I were sharing my deepest, darkest secret. This was something scary, in my opinion. Telling him that I was happy and him telling me that he was content didn't make this feel like a contract marriage. In all honesty, I hadn't thought of that piece of paper in weeks. If I wasn't careful, if we weren't careful, we'd get to our five-year mark with feelings we hadn't planned on having. We'd be walking away with broken hearts and I didn't want that. Shaking the thoughts from my mind, I refused to allow fear to drive my decisions. I cared about Zane and he was quickly becoming my best friend. I wasn't going to worry about what might happen. All I could do was live each day like it was my last and pray that my heart was intact when this was all over.

* * *

After realizing Sandro cleaned up the mess in the kitchen, and we changed into dry clothes, I took some cleaner into the basement to get the egg off Zane's chair. I noticed Sandro in the corner and had the urge to throw something at him again.

"You're going to get wrinkles from glaring so much."

"Oh, shut up, Sandy," I said as I wiped down the chair.

"I feel like Ivy might be your middle name," he said with a straight face.

"It's not."

"Are you sure your first name isn't Poison?"

"Poison Ivy? Really?" I wrinkled my nose. "Like I haven't heard that one before."

"Poison Ivy is irritating and itchy. That's how I feel about you sometimes."

"Sandy, I hate to break this to you, but that annoying feeling you get whenever I'm around means you like me. I get the same feeling when I'm with my siblings."

"You saying you look at me like a brother?" he asked, giving me a toothy grin.

"Currently, yes, but not if you keep staring at me like a creeper. I'll definitely look at you more like that weird cousin that lives in his mom's basement with all his pet rabbits."

Sandro's laugh filled the room. "You do not have a cousin like that."

"I personally don't, but I bet someone does."

"You're such a little dweeb," he said before heading up the stairs ahead of me.

We'd just reached the living room when I heard Zane yell my name from upstairs. "I swear," I said to Sandro. "If I don't get insane leg muscles from living here, I'll be very disappointed."

He gave me a weird look, and I gaped. "There are three floors! The massive amount of stairs are what I'm referring to."

He chuckled as I made my way upstairs and found Zane in our bedroom.

"You rang?" I said in a horrible southern accent. He smiled and motioned for me to take a seat beside him on the bed.

"I was thinking about what we talked about in the pool." I felt butterflies swarm my stomach, remembering the kiss, and when Zane smiled down at me I knew he was thinking the same thing. "Not that kind of talking."

"Oh my gosh," I, unfortunately, blushed. "Just tell me why you yelled across the entire house for me."

"Right," he pulled out his laptop and opened it, showing me a picture of the Grand Canyon. "How would you like to go see this in person?"

I looked between the computer screen and his face, my eyes wide, trying to figure out if he was being serious. "You want to take me to the Grand Canyon?"

"What do you say?" he asked.

Really? I had to ask? "Please?"

"What?" he laughed, "No, I mean what do you say, as in, do you want to go or not?"

"Oh," I smiled. "Yeah, I want to go!"

CHAPTER TWENTY-ONE

Ivy

The week leading up to our trip to the Grand Canyon was the most fun I'd had with Zane since our insanely quick nuptials in Vegas. I received more stolen kisses than I thought possible and Zane's smiles frequented his gorgeous face; I'd finally convinced him to shave his facial hair so I could see his dimples every time. The day before we left, we were sitting in the living room, watching the television he finally purchased after I'd been dropping hints about it for days. I wasn't sure how much more obvious I'd have to get, but one day I woke up and a television had been delivered to our front door and a cable guy showed up and started working on the picture.

"There's nothing on, Ivy," Zane grumbled from beside me.

"You're surfing the sports channels. Of course there isn't anything on!" I exclaimed. I tried grabbing the remote from him for the tenth time, but he quickly pulled it out of my reach.

"I don't think so, little girl." He shot me a triumphant smile. I grinned back and batted my eyelashes. "Oh, no you don't. Those stinkin' eyelashes are what got me into this whole mess with the TV. They won't get anything else out of me."

My shoulders sagged as the only hope I had deflated. Times like this made me wish I had my mother's charm or my sister, Kelly's incredible green eyes. That kid could ask our dad for anything when we were growing up and, before anyone knew what was happening, the little weasel got what she asked for.

"Who's a weasel?" Zane asked, and I glanced up at him. His smile told me that I'd said something out loud and I laughed.

"My little sister, Kelly." I answered.

"Is she the one that was flirting with Sandro or the one with red hair?"

"She's the one with red hair. And incredibly beautiful green eyes." I huffed. Zane's shoulders shook with his amusement, so I elbowed him as best I could and laughed when I heard his grunt.

We sat in silence for a few minutes as he made his way through more channels that held neither of our interests before he asked more about my family.

"Why did she look so out of it while we were there?" I didn't need to ask who he was talking about because I felt my heart squeeze in response.

"She's gone through a lot, lately," I said.

"Do you want to talk about it or is this something you'd rather me leave alone?" I looked up into his eyes and saw his concern for my feelings on the matter. I trusted him, and that was precisely why I decided to tell him part of her story.

"I can tell you about it." I turned my body, sitting with my legs crossed, facing him, and began. "When Kelly was a freshman, she started dating this boy named Breton. He and his family were new to the area, and it was like fate wanted them to meet. Perfectly balanced. They became friends really quickly and I think, like, a month or less into their friendship they started dating."

"Your dad let her date?" Zane interrupted. I couldn't blame him because I'd been shocked, too.

"Yeah, my mom convinced him things would be okay. So, anyway, they started dating and were together for almost two years. They were months away from the end of their junior year when Breton went swimming in the middle of the night, alone, in a lake. Ohio is still really cold in April and the next morning my dad overheard a call on his police scanner, saying that there was a body that had been found at the lake." I paused, trying to control my breathing as I remembered my baby sister's face for the first few days after her best friend's death. It was as if she'd lost her reason for existing, and I hated it with all my heart.

"So, that was a while ago, right?" Zane asked, bringing me back.

"Yeah, a little over a year ago."

"She isn't healing." It was a statement, not a question.

"She wasn't healing, no. But at the beginning of the year, right around the anniversary of his death, his younger brother showed up and told my parents that he was worried about her. Apparently, she'd been going to this field out behind his parents' property and was talking to Breton like he was there. My parents got worried, of course. My mom went to school for psychology and so she got Kelly into some extensive counseling. When we were there, it was the first time in I can't tell you how long, that she was able to be around so many people."

"How did your parents not notice something was wrong?" he asked. I tried to ignore the accusation in his voice.

"You don't understand," I said, trying to defend them even though I'd asked myself the same question. "They have seven kids, careers, and on top of all that, Kelly didn't show any signs that something was wrong. She went on with her life and they thought she'd found a way to cope. My mom suspected something was going on for a while, but she was scared to push her over the edge."

"She should have pushed," he said with conviction.

"You say that now, but one day, if you have a daughter in a similar situation, you might not say the same thing. She's my sister and I didn't know she was holding on to her dead boyfriend. I really thought she'd found peace, so how bad of a sister does that make me? The important thing is that she's actually getting help now, and she's finding ways to cope and move on."

"I guess you're right." I looked up and noticed he'd paused our channel-surfing and let out a humorless laugh.

"How did this conversation turn so bleak?" I asked.

"I was asking about your family," he answered.

"Is it my turn to ask about yours?" I asked. I tried hard not to be offended by the fact that I had yet to meet his parents or sister, but it was getting hard.

"What do you want to know?" He seemed to stiffen as he asked, so I decided to keep the conversation as light as possible.

"You said your sister is in high school?"

"She is. Emma's a senior this year."

"Does she play any sports?"

"No sports. She does, however, like to sing. She's an incredible singer, too. Even if she'll never own up to it."

"So, the Landis family has a singer and an actor?" I laughed. "My poor parents had seven kids and didn't get so lucky."

"What makes you say that?"

"Well, Jake is going to be a police officer, so they got lucky there. And Parker owns a coffee shop, so he's good. Duke, my youngest brother and I seem to be cut from the same vine. We would rather laugh. Graham is going through a goth phase and poor Rosa. She's only thirteen and, according to her, she's already had three boyfriends."

"What about Kelly?"

I smiled. "She used to want to be a teacher. I always told her she should be an artist, but she wanted to inspire children."

"She should be an art teacher. They inspire."

I grinned up at him. "You're right, I'll text her later." I paused before adding, "Tell me about your mom."

"Well, she's always stayed home with us, even though she would have loved to go to college. She dropped out of high school when she got pregnant with me and married my dad, so college wasn't an option."

"She could always get her GED, if she still wanted to go to school."

He gave me a sad smile. "I don't see that happening, babe. That ship sailed a long time ago and my mom just never got on."

He didn't continue, and I didn't think he wanted to keep talking about his family, so I changed topics. "There are still a lot of really important things I need to know about you."

"What's that?" he asked.

"How do you feel about space travel?" I questioned and his laughter surrounded me like a blanket. I felt triumphant and snuggled closer to him, causing him to lift his arm and wrap it around my shoulders.

"Space travel." He stopped to think about it. "I think it's pretty cool."

"So you think it's real?" I was wide eyed and shocked.

"You don't?" He glanced down into my eyes.

"I have my questions about it," I admitted. "I've never personally been there, so I can't very well say that it's real, now, can I?"

"I guess not, but I don't know why anyone would lie about it."

"You can't believe everything you hear, you know. It's suspicious."

"You are absolutely insane," he whispered, looking back at the television. I laughed under my breath because, well, I did believe that we'd been to the moon. I just liked to goad people, and it usually worked.

"Wait," I yelled when he flipped past a movie. The girl on the screen had just been pulled from a body of water and she was unconscious. "They're about to do CPR. You need to take notes."

"How do you know-," he stopped talking when another girl on screen called an ambulance and started chest compressions.

"See how she tilted her head back a little, first?" I asked. "That's important, Zane. You have to open the airway so air actually gets into the lungs."

I felt his eyes on me and looked up. Irritated, I grabbed

his chin with my hand and turned his head in the direction of the screen. "Pay attention."

Within a couple of minutes, the girl that had once been lying motionless on the ground started moving and breathing on her own. Zane looked down at me again and I fought the urge to roll my eyes.

"If you ever get in a situation that calls for me to have to perform CPR on you, I'll do it and then kill you myself."

A laugh escaped my lips, and I moved out of Zane's grasp and stood. "Flattery will get you nowhere, Mr. Landis."

"Where are you going?" he asked, resting the arm that had been around me on the back of the couch. I watched as his muscled flexed and relaxed and he noticed my attention.

"I was going to go to bed." I said. I pointed toward the stairs. Like he wasn't aware where the bedroom was. He simply shook his head.

"Not yet."

"Zane, we're leaving really early tomorrow morning." I reminded him.

"Ivy, I know what time we're leaving. Come, sit back down," he ordered, and my eyes narrowed in annoyance.

"Not until you ask nicely," I countered.

"Ivy." His voice had gone dangerously low, and I started to feel a giggle bubble up inside my throat.

"Zane," I said, breathing through the urge to laugh. "I know it must have been rough being raised as a barbarian, but you can't just demand things. Use manners."

The muscles in his arms bulged, signaling that he was about to pounce, and my feet took off running before my mind had time to catch up. My laughter rang out throughout the empty house and no one was there to save me from the man that I knew wasn't far behind.

I raced up the stairs and almost made it to the bedroom when I felt strong arms grasp my middle and swing me in a circle. I let out a mixture of a scream and a laugh, trying not to pee or pass out.

"If Sandro comes over here because you're screaming, I'm going to fire him." He kept one arm around me and started tickling my side with his other hand.

"Let me go," I laughed.

"I don't think that was the polite way to ask," he chuckled.

"Please!" I squealed.

"Why are you always trying to run away?" He asked as he sat me on my feet. He grasped my arm and turned me so I faced him, then reached up and pushed my hair away from my face.

"I don't know," I blushed. "I think it's fun, I guess."

"I think you just like it when I chase you."

I didn't answer because, deep down, I knew he was right. I knew he'd catch me every single time, but I didn't care. Almost every time, we'd laugh and goof around for a while and for some reason, those moments meant more to me than if we would have been hours deep in conversation about our hopes and dreams. I connected with him more when we were laughing and having fun.

My heart was beating faster in my chest, and I lifted my hand to his chest. I could feel every beat as if it mirrored my own. I looked up into his eyes, begging him to kiss me again. He got the message.

His warm lips covered mine in a soft kiss. His hands grasped my sides and brought me even closer, so I wrapped my arms around his neck. He lifted me easily and turned so my back was against the wall. The kiss was slow and sweet, nothing like the one we'd shared in the pool, but it held just as much passion. I felt so much joy as I shared this beautiful moment with my husband, the man that was so quickly becoming my best friend.

Zane broke the kiss, and I slid down until I was standing on my feet again. There was a second of disappointment, but then I remembered I had five more years of possible moments like this one.

"Baby," Zane said, drawing my attention to where he now stood in the closet.

"Yeah?"

"It was a bad call on the TV." He grinned and I rolled my eyes. I crawled into the bed, leaving the blankets folded down for my husband and basking in the tingling feeling that still covered my lips.

CHAPTER TWENTY-TWO

Zane

I was sitting alone in my office, grinning like a madman. I was looking through the pictures Ivy and I had taken on our trip and couldn't fight the urge to smile at every single one. I'd captured a few of her when she wasn't watching me, and those seemed to be my favorite. One, in particular, I wanted to blow up and hang on my office wall so I could look at it every single day. We'd just arrived at the Grand Canyon and she was looking out over the rocks with the most peaceful expression. She looked serene, and I craved that in my life. She made me feel like it was something I could actually have. In twenty-three years, I'd only known darkness, and she was like a candle. The light that I'd been praying and hoping for.

I remember the first time I felt the darkness that would become a constant home for my mind at twelve. The very first blow was in the stomach, but it was my heart that held the worst of it. The scars left on my heart were still painful, and it was something I vowed to keep inside me. I could take whatever it was the world threw at me, I just had to bottle it up and store it away where no one would find it. It was the latter that was getting hard. Ivy seemed to chisel away at the safe that held my secrets, and I wasn't sure how much longer I had before she'd completely break it down.

Her lips on my cheek pulled me out of my thoughts. I was still sitting in my desk chair starring at her photo on my laptop. Her arms wrapped around my chest from where she stood behind me and her nose pressed into my neck.

"Why are you still in here?" she asked.

I closed my laptop and pulled her arms away, leading her around to the front of the chair and guided her into my lap. "I was looking at our pictures," I answered.

"Looked more like you were staring at me, if I'm being honest," she said, and I chuckled.

"I guess it looked exactly like what I was really doing, then."

Her cocky smile made it impossible for me to resist the urge to push my fingers through her hair and bring her face closer to mine. She kissed me willingly, and the ache I had in my chest convinced me I needed more of her. I broke away and looked into her eyes, trying to see if she felt what was between us as much as I did.

"Ivy," I whispered. My voice was deeper than usual, and the slight raise in her eyebrows told me she heard it as well. "Ivy, I want to be with you."

She smiled. "You are with me, silly."

I returned her smile. "No, baby, I mean I want to be with you. I want to be your husband in every sense of the word. I don't want to leave anything out of our marriage anymore."

I saw the moment she understood what I was trying to

say, and the fear that flashed in her eyes forced a physical reaction inside my soul. It hurt to know she was afraid of me.

"Zane." Her breathing became a little irregular, and she stood, putting some space between us. I didn't stand because I didn't want her to run, but I grasped the armrests on the chair to hold me in place. "I, um. Good grief." She let out a humorless laugh and pushed her hands through her hair, an obvious sign of stress.

"Please, tell me how you feel," I begged.

"It's not that I don't want that, because I do, but," she paused and looked at me from where she stood. She straightened her back and shoved her hands into the pockets of her sweatpants. "Can you tell me, right now, that you're in love with me?"

Her question was bold. I envied that. I wanted to be bold like her; I wished I could take someone by the shirt collar and demand answers I needed. I thought about her question and then felt darkness ebb into my vision. I answered honestly. "No."

She flinched, and I almost changed my answer so she wouldn't feel pain, but it wouldn't be fair to her. She was my best friend and I couldn't imagine anyone ever being closer to me than she was, but I didn't know what love meant. Love had always been a very demented picture in my head, and what I felt for her looked nothing like the love that I knew.

"I'm not expecting you to love me, but love is something that is important to me. My husband and I will be in love. Then, and only then, will be the moment I become a wife in all ways. I don't want to hurt you, and I don't want you upset with me. I know you said there would be absolutely no cheating, and I hope you plan to keep that promise, but I can't be that for you." She was stuttering and sucking breath inside her lungs every few seconds. It looked like she was about to have a panic attack. I felt like a jerk for bringing anything like this up. I wanted to mend whatever trust I'd just broken between us. I'd promised her that this would never be a problem and not even three months into our marriage, I broke that promise to her.

"I'm sorry," I said. My voice cracked, and she looked like she was afraid I might cry, so I gave her a smile. "I'm sorry I brought it up."

"Don't be sorry!" she said. She slowly walked back over to me and got comfortable in my lap again. "I'm sorry I said no, I just need those things before I can take the next step."

"I understand. No matter how I feel, I would never want you to compromise yourself. You want and need those things and you completely deserve to have them." We sat in silence for a few minutes, listening to each other breathing since it was the only sound in the room.

"On a scale of one to ten, how awkward do you feel?" I asked when I couldn't take the silence anymore. Ivy started laughing hard, and I joined her.

"Oh, it was a level ten situation, like, five minutes ago."

"How do we move on from this?" I laughed.

"Well, we could go swimming," she suggested.

"It's raining." I sighed.

"Movie?"

"Raining."

"What?" She sat up and looked confused. "What does rain have to do with watching a movie?"

She must not have noticed the cable was out, and, for some reason, it made me smile. "Well, apparently the rain was too much for the cable to stand against and now we don't have a signal."

"You have got to be kidding me."

"Nope."

"But the internet works." She pulled out her new phone and pointed to the bars, proving that she was right.

"The internet is a different company, but beyond that, I can't really tell you why it's working."

She thought about it for a minute, then her beautiful smile turned into something I'll admit scared me a little. "Want to prank Sandy?" She asked.

It didn't matter if I didn't want to prank him. The grinning girl sitting in my lap was getting whatever she wanted, and she wanted to prank her bodyguard. So that's what we were going to do.

"What did you have in mind?"

"Glue on the toilet seat?" She laughed.

"What?" I exclaimed. "No!"

"What about pouring vegetable oil on his tailpipe so he thinks his car is on fire?"

"What in this world is wrong with you?" I asked. She started laughing like crazy, and I was really worrying about myself. I couldn't believe I'd married this lunatic.

"I was just kidding," she assured me.

"What are some pranks you pulled when you were younger?"

She looked embarrassed.

"You did not do either of those things." It shocked me.

"I've got an idea," she said, changing the subject so she didn't have to own up to my statement. "Do we have any food coloring?"

"I think so, but I'm afraid to ask why."

"Well, we can either put it in his toothpaste or in his shampoo. Your call."

I decided right then and there that I would never understand her need to play tricks on people. I hadn't even done anything yet, and I already felt bad. "Let me just say, if you ever pull something like this on me," I paused for dramatic effect. "I promise you on the contract that this marriage is built on that I will shave off both your eyebrows."

My threat had the opposite effect, because instead of promising that she'd never do it, her laugh was so loud that I jumped.

"I don't see anything funny about that." I said.

"Oh, my dear, dear husband." She said, still laughing. "What makes you think I've never had my eyebrows shaved off in retaliation before?"

"You're joking." She had to be lying.

"I have four brothers and two male cousins. My eyebrows have been put through the wringer a few times. It's okay though. I'm a beast at drawing them on, now." It took a minute for me to be able to absorb the information she just threw at me, but when it did, it made sense.

"Toothpaste. We'll put it in his toothpaste."

She gave me a goofy grin before standing and bolting off to the kitchen. I sat in astonishment that she could be so joyous about causing someone an annoying issue. Sure, it wouldn't hurt him, but he'd be really annoyed.

"Baby!" I yelled. I caught up with her in the kitchen. "Let's not mess with the toothpaste."

"Why not?" She looked bummed.

"I have a better idea. How about we go to the store tomorrow and buy a bunch of alarm clocks? Then we can set them for all kinds of crazy times and hide them all over his apartment."

"Wow," she said, walking closer to me. "I don't know if I've ever been this attracted to you."

I laughed as she kissed me on the lips and then pulled away. "Good to know."

THAT NIGHT when we went to bed we agreed to buy at least ten alarm clocks. Sandro was going to have a really bad day, if Ivy had anything to say about it.

She rolled over so her back was to my chest and I pulled her close, wrapping my arms around her, promising myself that I'd protect her as long as she let me. It was days like that, that reminded me she was such a young person at heart and I wanted her to stay like that as long as she could. She could find happiness in almost any situation. On top of that, she could make anyone around her feel the joy she felt. It was like that was her personal gift, to emanate joy. I craved it, now. When I wasn't around her, I felt like if I didn't find her, I'd be lost in the dark recess of my mind forever. But then there she was, walking through the bedroom or into my office, my own little candle, and all her light would take up the place the darkness once held. She chased it away, as if it were afraid of her.

My last thought before falling asleep was that if love could feel like this, then that's something I wanted. It was something I wanted more than anything else.

Shadows and nightmares have a way of sneaking up on you, though, because around two o'clock in the morning, my own personal nightmare called my cell phone.

"Hello?" I answered. I don't know why I picked up the call. I knew what it was about.

"It's happening again," the voice said. I heard the terrified scream before the line went dead and I was up, running through the house like my life depended on it, because unfortunately, a life did depend on it.

CHAPTER TWENTY-THREE

Ivy

I knew the moment Zane got up from the bed and I was still awake when he arrived back at home. I couldn't ignore it anymore when I heard the yelling.

I wasn't going to let things go this time.

I quietly walked to the basement stairs and descended them slowly. I didn't want to catch Zane's attention, and I successfully made my way over to a corner and sat down, bringing my legs toward my chest so I could rest my chin on my knees. I wrapped my arms around my legs and silently cried as he punched and kicked the bag that hung from the ceiling. I wanted to approach him so badly, but I was still scared that he wouldn't see it was me past his rage.

Zane had blood running from his upper lip. I assumed he'd been hit hard since there was a cut across the top of his nose as well. Thankfully, that was the only wound I saw and I wish it would have made me feel better, but it didn't. I ran through so many things in my mind, trying to figure out what it was that was going on. Was he fighting for money? Fun? Was he involved in something really bad and couldn't get out? Was he doing drugs again? Every question only brought on more, so I forced myself to stop. I'd get my answer the next time he left the house.

Sandro walked into the basement and looked around before spotting me in the corner. He pointed his finger upstairs, and I shook my head no. I absolutely refused to leave him. I couldn't.

"Get her out of here," Zane demanded. His voice was hoarse, it sounded almost painful for him to speak.

"No!" I yelled. I don't know who I was yelling at, but neither of them listened. Zane turned around so he couldn't see whatever happened next. And I'm glad he did. Sandro, my best friend, walked over to me and grabbed me, throwing me over his shoulder, and carried me upstairs. I pounded his back with my fists and cried, begging him to let me go so I could go back down to him. When he finally sat me down on my feet, we were standing in the living room and I pushed him away from me.

"I need to be with him," I said through clenched teeth. I felt so betrayed.

"I don't care what you think you need. He wanted you out of there," he answered. I moved to get past him and he grabbed my arm, keeping me there.

"Let go of me!" I sobbed. I stopped moving when I heard Zane's yell from the basement, then tried harder to get back to him when he stopped. "Please, just let me go to him, Sandy. He's hurting."

"I can't let you down there." His voice was full of authority and I hated it. I glared at him.

"You're supposed to be my friend."

Anger flashed in his eyes. "In this moment, I am an employee. I'm here to keep you safe and that's exactly what I'm doing!"

"Then get out!"

"You can't kick me out." His hand tightened on my arm. I tried to stomp on his foot, but he quickly maneuvered me, so my arms straightened behind my back. He pushed as far away from his body as he could get me.

"That hurts!" I yelled.

"Stop acting insane, Ivy!" he yelled right back at me. "I can't let you down there and if you don't stop fighting, I'm going to have to knock you out or something. I don't feel like wrestling with you while your husband is downstairs hulking out. I'm not entirely convinced I could take him when he's in this kind of mood."

"Fine." I exhaled a pent up breath when he released my arms. I turned and saw that he was ready to pounce on me if I made a move toward the basement door, so I walked away.

SANDRO FOUND ME, an hour later, sitting on the bedroom floor folding laundry through my tears. He came in and sat across from me, picking up a towel and helping.

"I think he's going to end up leaving again tonight," he said a few minutes later.

"What makes you say that?" I asked.

"He wasn't as banged up. Every time he came back with a bunch of gashes all over him, it seemed like he had a couple of nights off."

"You noticed that, too?" We'd stopped folding and were staring at each other like we'd just solved a piece of the puzzle.

"Why don't you know what's going on?" he finally asked.

"He's a closed off person, Sandro. We didn't date long," I looked at my hands that held a pair of his shorts. "I didn't know a lot about him before we got married."

"I guess that makes sense."

"I haven't even met his family, yet," I admitted.

"Really?" he asked, and I nodded.

"So, I have an idea," I said. I braced myself for rejection. I didn't know what I'd do if he said no, but I had to give it a try. "I think tonight we need to follow him. I'm going to call my dad and ask his advice, but I want to figure out what's happening to him."

"I agree," he said. My head jerked back in astonishment. I'd been prepared to argue until he gave in, but I didn't think he would simply approve of my plan.

"I think you should call your dad first," he suggested.

"I thought so, too, but I'm scared he'll freak out."

"It's not like he can get here and stop you," Sandro pointed out.

"Well, knowing him, he'd call the closest precinct and have them arrest me."

"Ah, yeah. That would certainly put a kink in our plans."

"Maybe I'll call him after we leave," I thought aloud.

"Much better." He stood to leave.

"Sandy," I said, stopping him. He looked down at me, and I had to tilt my head back to meet his eyes. "I'm sorry about freaking out on you. I appreciate you being here, helping me now."

"Don't worry about it, Sis." He smiled. "Just promise me when Zane gets back to normal you won't let him fire me for what we do tonight."

I returned his smile with a wobbly one of my own. "I promise."

* * *

IT WAS NEARLY midnight when I heard the front door slam shut. Since I already had my shoes on, I ran and met Sandro at his car parked inside the garage. I quickly dialed my dad's number and prayed he hadn't accidentally turned it on silent or something.

"Hello?" he answered. He was already asleep, but I didn't feel guilty for waking him. He told me, my entire life, if I needed him he'd be there, and I was really counting on that.

"Hey, Dad. I need you to listen because I don't really know how long I'll have to explain everything."

"Go." He must have heard the urgency in my voice because he was wide awake, now.

"A little over a month ago, Zane started coming home with cuts and bruises all over his body." I expected him to interrupt, but he didn't. "Every other night for two weeks, he'd show up at home with fresh wounds, but then it just stopped. According to his agent and staff, he does this a few times a year. Dad, I don't know what's going on! It started again last night and Sandro and I noticed a pattern."

"Tell me." I heard rustling in the background, and my mom was talking in a hushed voice.

"When he comes home really beat up, it's like he has a few days' rest or something, but when he isn't too bad off, he goes right back out the next night. I don't know if that makes sense at all, but that's what happens."

"It's okay, just keep talking."

"So, when this happened last time it took him, like, three

weeks to get back to normal. He was so angry, and he refused to even talk to me. It was so weird. I mean, he's already kind of broody, but this was so different. He stayed in the basement for a few days before he had to come out and when he finally came out, I was able to get through to him, I think. I don't know what all I'm saying right now. I'm shaking and confused, and I think I'm just rambling."

"So, what happened tonight? Did he hurt you?"

"No! He's never hurt me. I called because last night he got a call in the middle of the night and left. Then, this morning, he showed up at home with what, I think, might be a broken nose. That was the worst of it. He didn't look bad, but he left again tonight. Just a few minutes before I called you, actually."

"You're following him," he said when he realized.

"Sandro and I are following him, yes." I admitted. "Dad, I'm so scared for him. I'm scared I'm going to catch him doing something illegal, but I can't take him getting hurt anymore."

"Is he still driving?"

"He just pulled into the driveway of a house." Sandro answered for me. I felt nerves flutter in my stomach and thought it was a good thing I hadn't eaten anything because I'd probably be throwing up.

"Don't go in. Pull up where you're at on your map and text me the address. I'll see what I can find on the owner."

Sandro turned off the headlights as soon as Zane got out of his car and ran inside. He didn't even knock. We did what my dad asked and waited in silence as he did whatever it took to figure out who lived inside.

"Please hurry." I begged.

"Ivy," He paused. I looked at Sandro and he noticed the change in my dad's voice as well because he was frowning.

"What is it?" We were wasting precious time, and I was getting irritated.

"The house is registered to a Richard Landis." I felt a weird heat flood my body when the name registered. I thought back to that night that felt like so long ago but, in reality, was only a few days at the most. I'd stumbled upon a picture of him and his family when he was a teenager. I laughed because he looked so mean, even back then, and he gave me such a sad smile and said, "If I hadn't been mean, I wouldn't have survived."

I thought he was referencing everything that happened with his career, like the idiot I am. I thought he meant he wouldn't have survived his drug addiction or the fact that social media and entertainment news threw him under the bus, abandoning their so called beloved star.

"Ivy, does that name mean anything to you?" Dad asked.

"Yeah," I whispered. I cleared my throat and spoke louder. "Yes. That's his dad's name."

"Listen to me, Sandro, I'm talking to you. Don't you dare let my kid out of your car!" His voice was stern and the minute I heard the last word, my door was open and I was out, making my way to the front door. I took my dad off speaker. I left him on the phone in case something happened that he needed to hear and placed the phone in my back pocket. I felt Sandro beside me and readied myself for his grasp, pulling me back to the car, but it never came. I looked up at his face that held so much concern.

"You love him," he said and shrugged his shoulders. "Tonight, I'm here as your friend."

"My best friend," I corrected, and he nodded.

We walked to the front door and opened it without hesitation. Nothing could have prepared me for what I would see. I knew that something bad was happening, but I never would have expected to see Zane on the floor, shielding his face, as the man from the picture delivered kick after kick to anywhere he could reach with his booted foot.

CHAPTER TWENTY-FOUR

Ivy

My initial thought was that Zane could take his dad down if he wanted to. So why wasn't he? I looked around the living room, my heart racing, but nothing made sense. His mom and sister were sitting in a corner crying. Neither of them made a move to help Zane or stop his father. Zane was clearly not unconscious because he held one arm in front of his face and one near his ribs. Nothing made sense.

Richard stopped kicking and stumbled away to a table. He was mumbling something under his breath, but I didn't hear it, and when he lifted a beer to his lips, things started to register in my mind. I was fortunate enough to never have had an encounter with someone who was drunk, but just one glance around the room, and my experience with Zane, told me this was normal.

I wasn't thinking; I know that. But when Richard made a move toward Zane, I ran as fast as I could and threw myself on his body, receiving the kick meant for him. His foot connected with my hip and I felt so weak when I yelped from the pain. Zane jerked and sat up quickly. He only allowed himself shock at my presence for a moment, before anger like I've never seen filled his eyes.

I'd witnessed Zane's anger and wrath. Every morning in the basement for a few weeks he'd unleash this beast within him, but this was something new. It sent chills down my spine and I was helpless when he stood, leaving me on the floor.

Each step he took across the room was full of purpose and when he reached his father, he picked him up by the shirt, from where Sandro had placed him on the couch. I hadn't even noticed Sandro making a move for Richard. All I cared about was my husband.

"You messed up, old man," he said. His strained voice held more than just anger.

"Is that the wife you've been keeping away from us, son?" his dad asked. His words were slow and slurred. "Maybe I should press charges for trespassing!" Spittle flew from his mouth as he yelled, but Zane answered his question with a fist. I heard the crack of bone as his knuckles connected with Richard's jaw.

"My wife was none of your concern until you touched her, but now?" Zane laughed darkly. "Now you have a lot more to worry about than someone trespassing."

His mom ran over to where Zane was standing and tried to pull his hands away from his father. "Zane, honey, let your dad go, okay? We can work all of this out."

I'd forgotten she was even here and the minute I saw her, I was angry. She'd let her husband brutally attack her son for however long this had been happening. From the moment I sat down on a plane, leaving Ohio, I knew there was something inside this man that needed me. I may not have been the best at comfort or knowing what to do, but I knew I could be there for him. And even if I couldn't physically protect him, I wanted to. I would go to the gym and get strong, take lessons on how to fight, and learn how to be tough just so I could protect him. I hated his mom because she'd never protected him.

"Sandro," Zane said, throwing his dad back onto the couch. "Don't let him up."

"Yes, sir," he answered.

"Zane!" His mom grabbed his arm and tried to get him to look at her, but he only had eyes for me.

"Are you okay?" he asked. When I nodded, his expression looked angry. "Why'd you follow me?"

"I needed to stop whatever was happening to you. I couldn't take watching you go through this again. Please don't be upset with me, I just wanted to help you."

Surprise flashed in his eyes and he pulled me to his chest, wrapping his arms tight around me. A sob escaped me at the same time I remembered my dad was on the phone. I'd barely pulled away from Zane when I heard the sirens. He looked down at me, clearly confused. I pulled my phone from my back pocket and held it to my ear.

"Dad?" I said, and a sigh of relief answered. "Everything is going to be okay."

"Good grief, Ivy. I've been suffering a heart attack over here!"

"I'm sorry."

"What's going on? I called the local PD, are they there?"

"They just got here," I said, looking out the front door at

the seven officers that were standing in the lawn. "Dad, what the heck did you tell them?"

"I didn't know what was happening. I told them that my daughter was in there and I needed someone to go and get her."

"Okay, well, they're here now. I guess I should go."

"Listen, your brother and I are flying out in the morning. Mom booked the flight right after you called. The thing is, your mom doesn't think she should leave Kelly right now. She's been doing so well and she doesn't want her to be alone in case she takes a step back."

"I don't expect either of you to come, but I appreciate it. Tell Mom I understand that she needs to stay home."

"I knew you would, kid. Alright, I'll see you sometime tomorrow. Hey, make sure you tell them every single detail about what you saw. Don't you dare hold anything back to protect anyone."

"I promise." I whispered. Even if he hadn't said those words, I'd do it. I wasn't holding anything back.

We hung up, and I felt Zane's presence at my side, so I glanced up and flinched. His lip looked bad.

"You don't ever say, 'goodbye' when you're on the phone," he commented. I don't think he really meant to say it out loud, but I reached for his hand and held it tightly in mine.

"We've never done that. It feels weird to tell them goodbye."

"I like that." He pulled me closer, and that's how I stayed throughout the entire conversation with the officers. They asked what we were all doing there, and I was completely honest about following Zane. I told them that this is something that had been happening a few times a year for a period that I wasn't certain of. Zane refused to press charges against his father for any pain he'd suffered, but told me the kick to my hip was up to me. I knew he'd be arrested if I pressed charges, and since he was still trying to argue with Sandro a few feet from where I stood, I decided it was best to get him out of the home.

I wasn't a huge fan of Zane's mom or sister, but I wasn't about to leave them here with Richard when he was so angry.

Zane stood on the porch as his dad was placed into the backseat of a police cruiser, and I stood helplessly beside him. I didn't know what to say or what to do. I didn't know how he felt about Richard, although I knew that the one time he'd talked about him he'd had venom in his voice.

I was at a loss. I had a wonderful relationship with both of my parents and I didn't know how to act. One thing was certain, I wanted to cry hard, but I promised myself I'd save it for another day.

"Are you guys ready to go home?" Sandro asked.

I looked up at Zane and waited. Finally, he took a deep breath, and his eyes ran over my face before he answered. "You guys go home. I want to check on my family before I go."

I felt my heart seize up at the thought of leaving him. "I'll wait in your car. I want to be with you."

"Well, I'm not leaving until you do." Sandro said, looking at me.

"We'll wait out here, you check on them." I didn't say what I was thinking, that they needed to be the ones checking on him, but I think Zane saw it in my eyes. He looked sad, and I immediately felt like I failed him. He turned and walked back into the house, shutting the door behind him.

"You can't hate his family." I looked at Sandro and wanted to question him, but he held up a hand to stop me so he could finish. "You have no idea what has been going on in his life up until you came into it. You can't judge them or him for anything you saw today. Before you decide that you hate his family, maybe give him a chance to tell you his story, if he will."

"How can you not hate them?" I asked, tears welling in my eyes.

"Hate stirs up conflicts, but love covers over all wrongs," he answered. "Proverbs 10:12."

"Did you just quote the Bible?" I asked, smiling.

"I did. If you hate someone, all it does is make you miserable, but loving people despite their wrongs, well, it gives you the power to let things go. Why would you want to hold on to anger? It doesn't affect them, it only hurts you."

"You sound like my uncle Jackson." I sighed. "But you're right. I guess I don't hate anyone, I'm just confused. How could a mom let that happen to her child?"

"Your mom grew up with a dad that would take a bullet for her and that made her the woman she is today. It made her the mom she is. Not everyone is lucky enough to have that kind of influence, though. Maybe Mrs. Landis has never had anyone try to protect her, so she didn't know how to be that person."

"I don't know, Sandy. It makes me sad to think that she's watched her son get beat and never called the police."

"Give him a chance to explain it to you, before you jump to conclusions about anything," he urged.

I nodded, then walked to Zane's car. While I waited, I thought about Sandro's words and tried to let the scripture seep into my soul. It was difficult, but I kept trying.

192

When Zane finally climbed into the car, I was confident that I could love her, despite what she'd allowed to happen. But then I saw his lip and felt hatred rise up in me again. I didn't want to let it go. She didn't deserve to have forgiveness or love from me. My husband was bleeding and it might as well have come from her hands.

CHAPTER TWENTY-FIVE

Ivy

When we walked into the house, Sandro immediately went up to his apartment and we were left alone. My body had stopped shaking sometime between his parent's house and ours. I knew if I could just get Zane home, I could protect him from everything and I guess at that moment, he was feeling the same way.

He walked to the fridge and put some ice in a baggie, wrapped it in a towel, and took my hand. We walked up to our bedroom, and he picked me up and placed me on the bed before kissing my forehead.

"I'm going to go get a shower, okay?" he asked.

"Okay," I answered. He placed the ice on my hip and then walked into the bathroom. I waited a while before following him in and sitting on the closed toilet lid. He peeked his head around the curtain and gave me a questioning look. "I couldn't be away from you." I explained.

He closed the curtain and finished showering while I sat

there. A few minutes later, I lowered my eyes as he stepped out and dried off. After wrapping his towel around him, he grabbed my hand and pulled me into the bedroom again, placing me right back on the bed. He sat beside me, and I tried to make eye contact, but felt emotions I'd been holding in bubble to the surface. I wasn't sure I'd be able to speak without crying.

"Yesterday you asked me if I was in love with you," Zane's voice cut into the silence and my heart hurt, not wanting to hear that he didn't love me all over again. "I think I might have lied."

"You might have lied?" I asked, extremely thrown off.

"When I was growing up, my dad would go on these drinking binges. It only happened now and then, but he'd just drink for days and days. My first memory of my mom getting hit was when I was about four years old. I was only a kid and I couldn't do anything about it. Then Emma was born, and I got older. Mom would lock us in my room when she knew Dad was coming home from wherever he spent his days drinking, then we'd hear the fighting. I never heard my mom talk back or even try to defend herself, it was just him screaming about things that didn't make sense to me at the time. Money, stress, and so on. Then one day, when I was thirteen, I couldn't take it anymore. I broke my door and charged out into the living room and plowed into my dad. My mom screamed for me to get away, but I fought him with all the strength I had. I wasn't as tough as I thought and he landed a pretty good hit to my head."

I was breathing hard and trying to ignore the tears running down my cheeks. Zane scooted closer and wiped my face with his hands. "Don't cry for me, baby. It's okay."

I shook my head, still unable to speak. I wanted him to

195

keep talking; I needed him to know I was here for him, so I grabbed his hands and remained silent.

"I started noticing it didn't matter who my dad hit. As long as he got the upper hand on someone, he'd eventually come back out of his haze and be normal for a while. The decent times in between, and the fact that I didn't see my mom black and blue for a while, was worth it to me. If I could go back, I would do it all over again." His eyes moved to the window where a light rain had started to fall. "One day my mom told me that no one had ever stood up for her since she was in high school. She was picked on because she was a heavier kid, and I guess she didn't have many friends because she was so shy. My dad noticed her though and thought she was pretty. He liked her, and she eventually fell for him, got pregnant at sixteen, and then her parents made her marry him. She didn't care because she loved him, but after two years of marriage, he got fired from his first job for showing up late. I was sick or something and they weren't getting any sleep so he didn't wake up on time. He got fired, and he felt like a failure, so he turned to the only thing he knew. His dad was an alcoholic."

I sucked in a shaky breath. "It wasn't your fault."

"I know that," he smiled sadly. "Neither of them have ever blamed me, but when my mom told me that story, I felt like the least I could do was protect her. Ivy, my dad isn't a bad person. There are days I can't think about him because it hurts so much. I wish he would open his eyes and see that we love him even though he hurts us. I wish our love was enough to bring him out of this addiction, I guess."

I watched a tear fall from the corner of his eye and felt my heart break again.

"When my movie made it big, I was shocked and excited.

I had more money than I ever thought possible, so after paying off my mom's house, I went wild. I tried losing myself and tried forgetting the pain I had. Little did I know, the path I chose was causing more pain. I ended up addicted to drugs and the entire time I was away; my dad was hitting my mom again. I abandoned her, and she was hurting because of me. I should have stayed around and protected her."

"Zane." My voice broke. "Why didn't you ever call the police?"

"We did once, before I was old enough to help my mom, I called the police, and they came over. My dad's uncle was a cop, though, so nothing happened. They told my dad to calm down, and they left us. He was so angry after that. I decided to never ask for help again."

I got up on my knees and wrapped my arms around his neck. I couldn't hold it in anymore, I let go and cried. I cried because no one had stepped in and helped his family. I was proud that Zane had stood up for the woman that he loved with all his heart. I could not understand why she let her young son stand up to his father the way she did, but I loved Zane for doing it. His arms wound around my back, pulling me even closer.

We sat like that for a while until I finally pulled away. Sitting on my feet brought me eye to eye with Zane, and I saw the wetness on his cheeks. Like he'd done for me, I wiped his tears away with my hands and softly kissed his lips.

"I don't expect you to say anything, but I need you to know that I love you, Zane." I whispered. I feared his rejection, but I couldn't allow my fear to keep him from knowing. He needed someone to openly love him, and I could do that. I wanted to do that. "I'm not exactly sure when it happened, and I'm so sorry I'm breaking the rules here. I just want you to know that you have one person in this world that loves you enough to stand in front of danger for you. I'd do it a million times if I had to."

Zane lifted his hand and tucked a strand of hair behind my ear and smiled.

"That's the thing, Ivy. I don't think I understood what I felt for you until you jumped on top of me, protecting me with your body." He paused, putting his hands around my waist, he pulled me until I was on his lap. "I chose to stand between my dad and my mom, but no one has ever chosen to stand between him and I. No one until you, but then he hurt you and I couldn't see past the rage I felt. I didn't understand it. I felt angry when he hurt my mom, but something inside me snapped when I heard you cry out. I felt like there was nothing on this earth that would stop me from killing him for touching what was mine. For hurting my wife. The wife that, somewhere along the way, I grew to love."

My eyes widened at his admission. "You love me?" I asked.

"I love you," he answered with a smile.

"What about our contract?"

"We don't have to worry about that right now," he said. I wish I could say it didn't hurt, but it did. I wanted him to say that he didn't care about the contract and that he wanted me to stay, but I guess I could take things one day at a time. All I knew was that I loved him and he loved me. I smiled.

"I want to be your wife, now, Zane." I said, hoping he'd understand what I was saying. His eyes told me he knew exactly what I meant, and he leaned in, not questioning my decision to be with him.

This kiss was my favorite. It was filled with love and heat and everything I knew I wanted to share with my husband.

His lips moved across my cheek and stopped when he got to my ear. "I never knew love could feel like this," he whispered before moving us to the center of the bed.

CHAPTER TWENTY-SIX

Ivy

I woke up to the sound of Zane's voice and I glanced over my shoulder to see him standing at the door, shielding whoever was there from my eyes. Glancing out the window, I noticed the sun was setting, and I sat up quickly, checking my phone to see what time it was. We'd been asleep almost all day.

"Who's out there?" I asked. He looked at me and smiled.

"Hey, Sis!" Jake poked his head in and his eyes widened before he grinned. "Why don't you get out here so you can see your favorite brother?"

My face heated in embarrassment. "Get out of my room!" I yelled, trying to laugh off my nerves. Zane chuckled as he shut the door and walked back across the room. He climbed up on the bed and leaned in toward me, taking my lips in a kiss. "Good morning, Ivy."

"I think you mean good evening." I smiled and returned his kiss.

"Yeah, we missed a few meals. We also have guests." He

laughed and fidgeted with my hair. "You should probably brush your hair."

"Let's hurry then. Knowing Jake, he's probably already found your video games and tried to play them."

"If he messed any of my things up, I can't promise he'll be able to walk away," he said, and I laughed.

"You might have fifty pounds on him, but I would put my money on my brother. He's been in Martial Arts since he was a kid, and then he moved on to boxing and things like that. Plus, he wrestled in school."

"I played sports. I put my money on me." He was confident.

"Okay, I'll make you a deal. If you take down my brother at some point while they're here, I will promise-,"

"You have to get a tattoo," he cut me off, smiling. "If I take him down, you have to get a tattoo."

"What if he beats you?" I asked.

"Then I'll get a tattoo."

I started laughing. "Zane, you're covered in tattoos. You adding to them isn't that big of a deal."

"I'll get something that represents my love for you," he whispered, and my heart picked up speed.

"Really?"

"Yeah, really," he said. We'd only been married a few months. I knew it was fast to fall in love, even if the guy is technically your husband. The time it took to fall in love with Zane didn't matter to me, though. I wanted Jake to wipe the floor with Zane tonight so I'd have to see him get a tattoo symbolizing his love for me.

"Okay," I agreed. He smiled and sealed our wager with a kiss.

I showered and got dressed before bolting down the

stairs and ran into the living room where I found my dad, Sandro, and Jake all looking at the television, trying to get a picture to come up.

"I told you it was a bad call," Zane whispered in my ear as he walked by and I rolled my eyes.

"Hi, Dad!" I said. He turned, and I ran into his arms, squeezing him with all my strength. As much as I wanted to get away from where I'd grown up, I missed my family. When I lived with Pop and Gram, I would get to see my parents and siblings at least twice a month, but I'd only seen them once since June. Being this far away from them was harder than I thought it would be.

"It's about time you woke up," Dad laughed. He walked over to Zane and pulled him into a hug, taking him by surprise. His eyes met mine over my dad's shoulder and I smiled encouragingly.

"How are you doing, Son?" he asked, letting him go.

"I'm good," he answered.

"Do you know how to get this thing to work?" Jake asked Zane, and they joined Sandro at the TV. My dad came and sat beside me on the couch and pulled me into his side.

"How are you feeling?" he asked quietly.

"I'm okay. My hip is a little sore, but other than that, I'm just glad I found out what was going on. Honestly though, I feel bad for pressing charges."

"That's to be expected. Guilt will come and go but you just have to remember, he did a lot more to other people than what he did to you."

"That's what I keep telling myself." I took a deep breath, willing myself not to cry over what Zane's family, and especially Zane, had suffered. "I was scared to leave him at home with Zane's mom and sister there."

"Personally, and coming from an officer's perspective, I think you did the right thing. I know it just happened so you are kind of shocked, but you can't keep dwelling on it. Just know you did the right thing and try to move on."

"I know." I sighed.

"You can't force him to keep reliving this, either. Let him know you're there for him if he wants to talk, but you can't bring it up and act like he's wounded. He doesn't seem like he'd appreciate that very much."

"You're right about that. He'd probably grow to hate me if I acted like that." I said, and Dad patted my shoulder with his hand. We watched the boys try to fix the TV for another few minutes before I grabbed the remote and changed the input setting. The picture came on and all three heads swiveled around to stare at me openmouthed. Dad chuckled, and I shrugged before getting up to go start lunch in the kitchen.

I walked into the kitchen to see Zariah, and Rayna seated at the island. I'd forgotten they were

"Hello, ladies," I greeted.

"Hello, Mrs. Landis." They both answered.

"You can call me Ivy." I reminded. I'd told them on multiple occasions, but Zariah was the only one who listened to me whenever her grandmother wasn't around to correct her.

"I was going to make some lunch for everyone. Will you both be staying?" I asked.

Rayna started shaking her head before I finished the question and rose to put her coat on. "No, thank you. We'll be going home, now, if you don't have anything else for us to do."

I hated having them work here. I liked them both, but having someone there to do my laundry and clean my house felt wrong. I would never suggest letting them go again because it was how they made money, but it was just something I was still having a hard time adjusting to.

"Why don't you stay, Zariah?" I asked and her eyes widened.

"Are you sure?" she asked, her pale cheeks turning pink.

"Of course! I'd love if you stayed."

"Okay." She nodded then hugged Rayna goodbye.

"Do you want help?" she asked, walking back into the kitchen.

"Sure! I'm not the greatest cook outside of breakfast food, so I need all the help I can get." I laughed.

"Well, this isn't good," she said, laughing with me. "The only thing I've learned to cook is peach cobbler."

"We're probably going to set off the fire alarm."

"I'd say chances of that are pretty good."

I opened the freezer and pulled out a couple pounds of burger and looked at her. "Spaghetti. We can't really mess that up, right?" I asked.

"I don't think so," she said. She sounded uncertain, but I chose not to comment on that, believing we could manage noodles and burger.

"Why haven't we done this before?" I asked while I put the burger in the microwave.

"Because I've been a jerk," she answered.

I gave her a questioning look. "You've never been a jerk."

"I have. I had a crush on Zane when my grandma let me start working with her. I was young and saw this celebrity, and then a few years later you show up out of nowhere. He never looked at me, let alone thought I was special. Then you came, and you became his whole world. He watches you when you're not looking, and I got jealous. I shouldn't have made it such a big deal, I'm sorry."

"Just because he was your crush doesn't mean that it wasn't a big deal, Zariah. You built someone up in your head only to be let down when they hadn't done the same for you, it's not uncommon." I said. "One day someone is going to see something really special in you and they're going to fall in love."

"Yeah, right!" she laughed. "The most I can offer is a clean house."

"Listen, a clean house isn't a small feat. My mom had about a hundred little brats running around and still managed to keep a tidy home. Plus, there's more to you than what you do for a living."

"Like what?" she asked. She sounded like she was really asking me what she could offer, and I felt so guilty that I hadn't made any attempt to get to know her better before this.

"Well, what do you enjoy?" I asked.

She thought for a minute before answering. "I love to write and read, but that doesn't really contribute to a relationship or a household."

"What's your fixation on contributing to a household, though? You aren't married yet, and that isn't a bad thing. You can enjoy your life and do whatever you want right now. If you love to write, then write. One day you're going to meet the guy that you'll end up marrying, but the best thing you can do for him is to make sure you do what's right for you. Make yourself happy right now."

"Is this what you wanted? To get married at twenty-one?" She asked, pouring the noodles into the boiling water on the stove.

"Honestly? Absolutely not. I didn't want to be married at all, to tell you the truth. I wanted to travel the world, but life is funny like that. I had all these plans and then I met Zane and really fell in love, and now I don't know what I want to do with the rest of my life." I paused, feeling saddened by my next whispered words. "I just know I want it to be with him."

"Maybe we should go to college," she joked.

"Maybe we should!" I said, and she looked at me funny. "I'm being serious! I didn't go to college because I worked for my grandparents, but I'd love to go and get a degree. You could go for a degree in writing or something."

She let out a sigh. "All this talk about my future is starting to freak me out."

"Sorry," I said, laughing. "In all seriousness, though, I think you really should look at yourself in a different light. You're a beautiful girl and you definitely deserve to be happy doing whatever you enjoy."

"Thanks, Ivy." She smiled, and we finished lunch, barely managing to not burn the meat.

* * *

"Lunch is ready!" I yelled to the guys from the kitchen. They all walked in and immediately went to the stove to scoop out a mountain of food onto their plates.

"Who made the bread?" Jake asked, motioning to the garlic bread Zariah made from a regular loaf of white bread.

"That was Zariah," I said.

"Wow! I might just have to take you home with me so I can eat like this more often." Jake said. I smiled at Zariah and almost laughed when I noticed her face was beat red. "Cute and can cook," he said to himself, walking back toward the living room.

Both mine and Zariah's eyes got huge as we looked at each other, and she was the first to crack a smile before turning around to hide it.

"Hey, Mr. Murphy," Zane started. "Do you think I could take Jake down in a fight?"

My dad looked at him and contemplated something before answering, "I guess it would depend on the kind of fight."

"Boxing!" Sandro yelled from beside me, causing me to jump. "You've got plenty of gloves, let's fight tonight."

"I don't know, Zane." My dad continued. "I think he might have you beat on skill, unfortunately."

"Agh!" he laughed. "I guess we'll just have to wait and see!" He wiggled his eyebrows at me before walking back into the living room.

* * *

AFTER LUNCH, while Zane and Jake cleaned up the kitchen, I sat with my dad in the basement. I laughed as Sandro taught Zariah how to play a game I'd never heard of. She kept shooting the wrong people, and he was getting frustrated.

"They're the ones in blue! Not gray!" he yelled, looking at the screen.

"Oh my gosh, Sandro. They're basically the same color!"

"No, they aren't," he grumbled.

"Is it always like this here?" My dad asked, drawing my attention away from my friends.

"Actually, not really. This is the first time it's felt this peaceful since I got here," I admitted. "It was a lot to get used to but on top of that, no one really got along. I had no idea Sandro was part of the deal, so I tried to fire him a few times."

"I'm glad Zane loves you enough to have someone living here and being paid to protect you," he said.

"Me, too. Sometimes I don't understand why he's here since Zane isn't in the spotlight anymore. He's trying, but nothing has happened. It doesn't really feel like he's famous or anything."

"He's a real person. I guess we forget that about celebrities."

"It was weird when the lady from that magazine came here for an interview, that's for sure. The couple of times we've been out, there were only one or two people taking pictures. Nothing too crazy, thank God."

"Your sisters think it's the most romantic thing ever." Dad laughed. "I told them if they did anything like this then I'd probably die an early death."

"Hey! I said I was sorry," I said, and he smiled.

"I know, I'm just giving you a hard time."

"So," I said after a moment. "How's Kelly?"

Dad sighed. "She's still doing about the same. Healing can be a slow process, and I think a slow process is exactly what she needs."

"She held on to grief so long that it's probably better for her to take her time."

"Exactly. I'm not a professional, but I really think she's much better than a few months ago."

"I think so, too. She looked great when we visited."

"She was happy to see you. Everyone was," he said and

smiled. "I hope you and Zane get to come back for another stay soon."

I didn't respond, but I hoped the same thing.

CHAPTER TWENTY-SEVEN

Zane

Sandro finally gave up trying to teach Zariah how to play a game and handed the controller to Ivy. He had more patience than I did, that's for sure. I'd refused to teach Ivy to play on more than one occasion simply because I didn't want to yell at her for not understanding what I was telling her to do.

Jake stepped up to the shelf where all my boxing gloves were and picked a pair out while Sandro talked to him. I decided to watch them fight first so I could see Jake's routine and get a feel for how I'd be able to beat him. I wanted to beat him. I wanted to watch Ivy get ink.

Whether Jake won or not, I'd be getting a tattoo. I'd set up an appointment as soon as Ivy fell asleep in my arms, the night she told me she loved me. I decided then and there to add to my chest piece.

"Come on, brother," Jake taunted Sandro.

"Take him down, Sandy." Ivy laughed and Jake's mouth dropped open.

"You aren't supposed to root for him! I'm your blood."

"Blood doesn't make you family," Ivy's dad said from the couch. He was reading the paper, not paying the least attention to what was happening ten feet away. I had no doubt, though, that if the guys got too close to him, Brennan could take care of himself.

"Exactly!" Ivy said before she turned around and watched Zariah shoot the wrong team again. I chuckled to myself when Ivy pulled her lip between her teeth and also shot the wrong team members. If they'd been playing with my few online friends, I'd probably get kicked off the team, but I made sure it was offline.

Sandro took a quick shot to Jake's head but was blocked by his left hand. They went back and forth and in the end I only learned that Jake knew what he was doing in a fight and I probably had no hope.

"You ready?" he asked, giving me a wicked grin. He had sweat pouring down his face and neck, and I tried to look at it as an advantage. Hopefully, he was tired.

Chances were small from the looks of it.

"Yeah, I'm ready."

The minute I stood in front of him, he took a cheap shot to my stomach and cracked me in the face in the next second. He started laughing and threw a look over his shoulder at the girls, who'd turned around to watch us. I grabbed his head under my arm and held him against my side while I repeatedly hit his ribs. He was punching anything he could reach and, finally; I let him go and pushed him away from me.

"Keep your eyes on me, Jacob," I teased, using the name

I'd only ever heard his mom call him while we were visiting Ohio. "Wouldn't want that pretty face of yours marred with bruises when you get home. Although, pity dates would be good for your ego."

"Oh, I'm not interested in dating anyone back home." He smiled crookedly and ran at me, tackling me to the ground.

We went back and forth, punching and kneeing each other wherever we could hit. He landed quite a few good hits, but I was keeping up. Jake grabbed a towel to wipe the sweat from his eyes and I took my chance, whether it was cheating or not, I didn't care. I grabbed him and pushed him down to the ground, shoving my knee into his spine. He tried to swing his arms at me behind his back, but I was too heavy for him to move much.

"Give up, bro." Ivy laughed. I didn't notice when she moved from the TV to the couch beside her dad, and I was thankful we didn't end up over there. Two grown men landing on her would have hurt.

"Okay!" Jake chuckled from below my knee. "You win, just get your fat butt off me."

"Fat?" My laugh boomed in the basement. "I think I might have less body fat than you do, buddy." I quickly stood and grabbed Jake's hand to pull him up when he flipped over.

He stretched and walked into the restroom that was beside my office, shutting the door behind him.

"What's the matter with him?" Sandro asked.

"He's such a sore loser," Ivy said, laughing. I looked around and noticed Zariah was missing before I walked to the couch and sat beside Ivy. I pulled her as close to me as I could and squeezed her.

"You're disgusting," she said, wrapping her arms around me, anyway. This is what I loved. It didn't matter that I was literally dripping with sweat and probably smelled awful. She wanted to hug me.

"You love me anyway," I teased. She looked up at me and smiled.

"True."

"Oh man, you guys are grossing me out," Jake said when he emerged from the restroom. "I've got to run out to the car. Be right back."

"We aren't as bad as Mom and Dad!" she yelled after him.

"True!" He started laughing halfway up the stairs.

"What's that supposed to mean?" Brennan asked, looking up from the paper he was still reading.

"Dad, you and Mom made us all want to throw up constantly with your kissing and hugging all the time. It was awful."

Brennan smirked at me and Sandro. "Her mom is hot, what can I say?"

"So, that's where you get it from?" I smirked at Ivy and Brennan narrowed his eyes at me.

"That's my kid you're talking about."

"You mean my wife?" I asked. I knew I was treading on dangerous ground, but now that I knew I loved her, I felt almost possessive. She was my family now.

I held Brennan's stare for almost an entire minute and was surprised when he finally smiled. "That's the kind of man I hoped you'd be."

"Glad I didn't disappoint," I grunted. Ivy's shoulders shook in laughter, and I lightly pinched her side to get her attention. She looked up at me and grinned, and I couldn't help but return it.

"So," I started talking, interrupting the peaceful silence. I was nervous about what I wanted to say, but I knew I had to do it. "I wanted to invite my mom and sister over for dinner, tomorrow night."

As soon as the words came out of my mouth, Ivy's body tensed like I knew it would.

"I don't think that's the best idea." Ivy stiffly said.

"Why not?" Sandro asked. He and her dad simultaneously gave her a weird look, and it seemed to make her body relax.

"Okay," she relented. I was almost jealous that they had that much persuasion over her with just a look, but I was also grateful. I loved my mom and sister, and I loved Ivy. Was it too much to ask that they all love each other, too? "Jake has to cook dinner tonight, though. He makes the best fried chicken and mashed potatoes. I'll go find him."

She stood and bolted up the stairs. She said she was looking for Jake, but I knew she was trying to get away from the conversation. Brennan gave me a sad smile.

"She doesn't like my family," I sighed.

"It's not that she doesn't like them, she just doesn't understand them. I don't mean any disrespect to your mother, but she can't comprehend that a mom wouldn't call the police if their-." He stopped the line of conversation he was on and took a deep breath before changing gears. "I grew up in foster care and didn't get adopted until I was sixteen years old. When I was around eight, I was with a family where the husband was abusive, and the wife never called for help. She was afraid of what he'd do when he got out and came back home. I didn't understand until I started having to respond to cases like that as an adult. It's easy to look in from the outside and judge someone, but it's not our place. All we can really do is be family. Know that you have a dad that loves you, a mom that would do anything for you and a bunch of siblings that will have absolutely no problem asking for money, and whatever else they can think of. You're part of our family and we love you."

I didn't know what to say to that. I had mixed emotions about the entire statement. On one hand, I felt like I was betraying my parents and sister by accepting that I was a part of Ivy's family. On the other hand, I almost felt like I could finally relax. Knowing people loved and cared for you was a strange sensation.

I knew my mom loved me, in her own way, and Emma only learned to stay quiet because that's what we'd taught her. I didn't blame them for anything; I was only angry at my father's demons.

"I appreciate that, Mr. Murphy."

"You can either call me Brennan or Dad. No more of this Mr. Murphy business," he chuckled.

* * *

AFTER JAKE MADE A DELICIOUS MEAL, everyone left to go to their separate beds, leaving me alone in the kitchen with Jake.

"You have to swear to me that you're going to teach Ivy how to make that," I said with a straight face.

He laughed but gave his word before going to the basement to sleep on the couch. I headed upstairs and overheard Ivy telling someone she loved them before hanging up.

"Your mom?" I asked, walking into the room.

"No, my cousin Cal. His leg is giving him problems, I guess."

"That can't be good."

"It's not. He finally got his cast off and then went and tried hiking a week later. He's an idiot."

"Honestly, that sounds exactly like something you would do."

"Are you saying I'm an idiot?" she asked with a grin.

"If the shoe fits," I said, joining her in bed. My entire body ached, and I couldn't wait to close my eyes and sink into oblivion.

* * *

"Zane?" Ivy said after what felt like a few minutes. I must have fallen asleep because the lights were now off, and the comforter was thrown across my body. I grunted in response.

"Are you awake?" she whispered. If my eyes would have been open, I would have rolled them.

"No, Ivy, I wasn't awake, but now I am," I said, letting my annoyance color my voice.

"Oh, okay. Sorry." She rolled over, putting her back to me, and I knew I'd hurt her feelings.

"Baby," I chuckled despite wishing I were asleep. She didn't answer, so I moved closer to her and pulled her back into my chest. I pushed one arm under her pillow and threw the other around her body, pulling her in even closer. "What's going on?"

"Nothing," she answered.

"So, you woke me up for no reason?" I asked.

"Apparently."

"Please stop acting childish and tell me what's wrong before you actually make me mad."

She huffed. "I just," she stopped talking and wiggled her body around in my tight grasp until she was facing me. "I feel like an idiot."

"Why do you feel like an idiot?" I could barely make out her face in the darkness, and I watched as her eyes moved back and forth between my own.

"Because I don't know what you need from me. I want to scream because of how you were raised. I want to destroy something because the rage and hurt I feel in my heart for you is tearing me up inside, but I don't think that's the right thing to do. I'm your wife and anyone that hurts you hurts me. If no one else will be a shield around you, then I will! But then I look at you, when you talk about your family, and I feel like you need me to be forgiving. You won't want me to speak my mind. You don't want my anger toward your mom and sister to be something we talk about at dinner, so what do you want me to do? Be silent?"

I mulled over her words for so long that she eventually closed her eyes to go to sleep. She was right though; I wanted her to be silent about how she felt about my family but, in my heart, I knew that wasn't fair. If roles were reversed and her family hadn't protected her when someone was hurting her, I'd be a raging bull destroying the world that hurt her, demolishing anyone that stood in my way. Even now, as her husband of a few months, I wished there was a way that I could ensure she never felt pain. I would take it all if I had to.

Ivy was strong. She was opinionated, and she was an extremely caring person. I thought back to the first time I came back from my parents' house, covered in cuts from a glass cup he threw across the room. She was so messed up for the few weeks that followed. She brought me food when she, herself, wasn't eating.

It felt like a dream, knowing how much she cared about me. Knowing she'd go to war with my family just to give them a piece of her mind. The only other time I remember feeling like this was when Trina had taken me to rehab and, with tears running down her cheeks, promised me it was for the best. She'd been right, of course.

I trusted Trina to do what was right for me back then, and I trusted Ivy now. I wasn't expecting her to save me, because that was my job, but I trusted her enough to know she would respect my love for my family. She'd speak her mind, saying all the things she wanted to say, in the nicest way she could.

And I could set aside my controlling attitude long enough to let her do it. She was my wife, and she had a right to the feelings she had.

CHAPTER TWENTY-EIGHT

Ivy
December

The house was complete chaos. It seemed like everywhere I looked, there was someone standing or sitting. It was Christmas, meaning it was my favorite time of year, and I'd invited everyone to fly out to our home. Zane offered to pay for their plane tickets, which I thought was incredible. Everyone came.

I ran down to the basement to grab a few folding chairs and halted as soon as I saw Pop. He was standing just inside Zane's office, looking down at a piece of paper. My heart started beating so hard that I had to force myself to take a deep breath.

"Pop?" My voice sounded strained when I spoke his name, but he looked up from the paper and waited. "What are you doing in there?"

"Zane told me to come look at his office. He said there

were a few car models I would like, and I accidentally knocked over his papers."

I knew he wasn't lying. "So, you picked them up," I said.

"Yeah, I didn't mean to read it, I just saw the words, 'marriage contract,' and felt my heart stop."

I walked into the office and shut the door, ensuring no one would overhear us. "Pop, it's not what you think."

"Then what is it?" he asked. He wasn't angry, but I could tell he felt confused and probably worried. "It says you get a million dollars if you stay married for five years. Are you planning your divorce already?"

"This is how it started, with the contract I mean. He asked me to marry him to help his image, but, we fell in love." I smiled, feeling the truth of what I was saying. "I love him more than I ever thought I could love someone."

"What about this thing?" he asked, holding the contract up.

"We haven't really spoken about it. I know I don't want a divorce. It doesn't say anything about fighting for the marriage, and to tell you the truth, if he wanted to honor the contract, I'd fight. I didn't plan on loving him, but I do."

"This is a lot to take in. I mean, your mom falling in love with a homeless man, even with me knowing who he was almost drove me crazy. I'm going to be worried about you for the next four and a half years now, Ivy."

"Please don't worry about me. I promise you, no matter what the outcome is, I won't regret this. Getting hurt is a possibility, but I don't think I will. Zane loves me and I don't doubt him for a second because you didn't see the man I lived with when I first got here. He was so dark and moody all the time, but little by little he started coming out of the darkness. It's almost like being here has helped redeem what was inside of him."

Pop sighed and walked to the couch to sit down. "I don't know what I'm supposed to do with this information."

"You can't tell anyone. It's supposed to be a secret, and if anyone ever found out about it, Zane's dreams would be destroyed. His image would be even worse."

"Ivy, I can't keep this secret from your grandmother. We don't have secrets."

I walked over and took a seat beside him, laying my head on his shoulder. "You can tell Gram if you want to. I understand that, but please keep this between the two of you. I really do love him, and even if I still have to leave after five years, I'll be okay because I knew I helped the man I love achieve something."

"That's being too selfless. You're not taking your heart or feelings into consideration. I told your mom so many times that you are the keeper of your heart, you need to be careful about who you let in."

Hearing the phrase he spoke to my mother, and she spoke to all us kids our whole lives brought a smile to my face. I don't know what we would have been without this amazing man. "You're the greatest, Pop. I hope you know that."

"Yeah," he sighed again, "I know."

I laughed and stood to go back upstairs, but paused by the door. "I can have Zane's agent call you and talk to you about this if it will help you feel better."

"I think that would help, absolutely." He stood and placed the paper in a drawer at Zane's desk, and I realized he was protecting us from the possibility of someone else seeing it. We made our way upstairs, and I realized I forgot the chairs.

"Where are the chairs?" Zane asked, coming up and pulling me into a hug. He kissed my forehead, and I glanced at Pop, caching his smile before he was lost in the chaos of our family.

"I forgot them. I actually need to talk to you, so let's go get them together."

When we got to the basement, I turned and looked at Zane. "My grandpa found our contract."

"What?" His face drained of all color and he looked like he might pass out. "What did he say?"

"He said he'd keep our secret, except for telling my grandma, which I get. I told him I'd have Trina call him to talk to him about it, though."

"Do you think he'll really keep it a secret?"

"There's not a doubt in my mind he will. He's harbored secrets for almost thirty years that I know of, so, I'd say your safe."

His eyebrows drew together in confusion. "Ivy, I don't just care about my image, I care about what would happen to you if anyone found out about this. You'd be a target and I can't imagine what would happen. I love you too much to risk that."

"I love you, too," I said, stepping into his arms. "I'm not worried about Pop, although we really should put that away somewhere so no one else finds it. It was just sitting on your desk."

"We'll put it in my safe," he said, walking into the office. He opened his safe as I got the contract from where Pop had placed it and handed it to Zane. After closing it, we both got a few chairs and went back upstairs to the party.

"Ivy, sweetheart, would it be alright if I went ahead and

started on the potatoes?" Zane's mom, Helen asked. I threw an arm around her shoulder and walked with her into the kitchen.

"Oh, for sure. Make sure you make all that you can find because I have a feeling they'll demand more if you don't. Don't tell my brother, but you make the best mashed potatoes."

"I heard that!" Jake yelled from across the room. We all laughed, and I helped gather some food that we were cooking for dinner. After handing Zane and Jake the burgers and hot dogs, I went back to helping Helen peel and dice the potatoes. The boys put their coats on and went out to put the meat on the grill, yelling the whole way about how cold it was outside and how they should let everyone starve. Everyone laughed, knowing they'd walk out there in just short if it meant they got to eat good food. They were the biggest eaters I'd ever met.

The weeks that followed our initial dinner, where I officially met Helen and Emma, were rough. I tried so hard to find a way to forgive them for what happened, but I didn't think it would be as hard as it was. Sandro helped a lot with his constant encouragement, and the fact that Zane wanted us all to be able to live in peace was a huge push, too. It wasn't until I spent a morning alone with his mom that my heart started to thaw towards her. We'd gone to breakfast together and throughout the entire meal, she asked for permission to ask me a question. Even as she ordered her food, it was like she was seeking approval for the meal she wanted.

The minute I noticed it, it was like it was a constant presence. It was always there, now. Her need to ask before she did something. She'd lived in this bubble for so long, having to live under her husband's thumb, that she forgot how to be independent. I didn't think she even realized that she asked anymore, and it broke my heart.

It wasn't that asking permission is what bothered me; it was the look in her eye, like she was waiting for rejection that hurt the most to see. Like a waiter really would tell her she couldn't have pancakes for breakfast or I would honestly refuse to allow her to get a glass of water from the kitchen.

Our relationship seemed to get better and better, though. She wasn't asking as often anymore, and I started seeing a flicker of light in her eyes now and then. The day that things sunk in for me, I decided I couldn't hate her anymore. What better weapon was there than love, anyway?

"Ivy!" Zane yelled a while later from somewhere in the house. I laughed when I saw my brother, Graham, roll his eyes and I stuck my tongue out at him. He thought he was so cool in his black clothes with his hair in his eyes.

"In here!" I yelled back.

"We got it!" he said. He was holding a box and my eyes turned huge.

We got the magazine.

"Oh, my goodness!" I was nervous. This woman had published our story and the only one who'd read it was Trina so she could make sure all the facts were correct. She said we needed to wait to read it, that we'd be really happy with it, so we waited. "Open it!" I squealed.

Zane tore into the box and pulled one out. "Who wants to read it?" he asked, looking around with a grin.

"I'll read it." My dad walked up and grabbed it from Zane. He opened it and started flipping through the pages until he came to a page that had a picture of me with my back to

Zane's chest. His face pushed down into my neck and his eyes were closed. I had a shy smile on my lips and my own eyes were on the floor. The blush they'd captured was a real one, I remember because Zane had just whispered something sweet to me before they took the picture.

"Alright," Dad started. He cleared his throat.

This past August I had the immense pleasure of sitting down with actor, Zane Landis and his beautiful wife, Ivy Landis. I would be lying if I said I hadn't been nervous, but the moment the brown-haired, grey eyed, brand new wife answered the door, I felt right at home.

Ivy's joy was infectious, and it was immediately apparent why someone could fall in love with her. When Zane finally joined us, I was star struck. This man was the one all the girls talked about when I was in college. Beautiful, blue eyes with short cropped blonde hair was something you just didn't want to look away from. I don't know what was happening that day, but Zane didn't look like an interview was something he wanted to do. He looked exhausted and almost a little irritated, but the moment he sat down beside his wife, it's like he came to life and was able to breathe. I gathered a lot from the interaction between them. A simple touch from his wife brought something out of Zane. Something truly beautiful.

When I think of newlyweds, I picture fawning and gushing over one another. This isn't the image I got from them, though. No, there was no excessive romance. No lingering glances or choreographed smooching. At one point, Ivy leaned over and kissed her husband on the cheek and had it not been for the genuine surprise in his eyes, I would have thought it was for me. For our readers. But it was only for them.

Have no fear! There was plenty of sweet romance and real love that

I was able to capture. I was fortunate enough to get the scoop on what goes on in the Landis home as well as what these two mean to each other, but first let's meet Ivy.

Ivy grew up in a small town in Ohio with her parents and six siblings. Granddaughter to Isaac Cooper II, owner of Cooper's Cars & Stuff, Cooper's, 'as everyone back home calls it,' is actually where these two love birds met. They fell in love over a flat tire and an open gas cap. And according to them both, it was love at first sight. I didn't believe in that before today, but now, I definitely do. This beautiful couple embodied love and companionship. If Zane moved, Ivy noticed, and vice versa. It was almost as if a string connected them and could sense what the other was doing. It's been a long time since I've witnessed something so beautiful. Like their relationship was a dance, and we were the audience. It was natural.

Dad smiled and looked up from the article at me. "There's more, but they're just the questions she asked. I figured everyone could read that on their own."

The minute the words left his mouth, everyone was flying at the box, pulling magazines out for themselves. Within seconds, it seemed, Callahan was laughing. "Ivy," he snorted. "He cuddles?"

Zane narrowed his eyes at me. "I thought you said she probably wouldn't put that in there."

"I lied," I laughed as he stalked toward me. "No one would keep it a secret that the menacing Zane Landis likes to snuggle."

"You're in trouble," he said. His lips pressed against my ear. His voice was low enough that only I could hear it.

"Bring it, big boy," I whispered back and his laughter made me smile.

"We've got to work at making you a little scarier, babe."

"I think you can be scary for the both of us." I stood on my tippy toes to give him a quick kiss on the lips, but his hand grasped the back of my head, holding me there. The kiss lasted long enough to get catcalls from a few people, but mostly my dad was yelling for someone to make it stop.

CHAPTER TWENTY-NINE

Zane
March

I don't know what Ivy's obsession with spring cleaning was all of a sudden, but she had Sandro and I helping her. She was in the living room hanging curtains on the window she hated and I was upstairs in my closet sorting through clothes. Apparently, I didn't need as much as I had.

"I don't understand why I have to go through my stuff," Sandro complained. "I don't even live in the house."

"I don't know, dude, just do it so we don't get yelled at again." She'd turned into a spitfire recently. Cleaning and organizing junk. Throwing away things I'd forgotten I even owned.

Ever since Christmas, when our families were here, I was beginning to feel differently about what I wanted my future to look like. I didn't like questioning the thing I'd worked so hard for, but I found myself doing exactly that. I didn't know that I wanted to act forever, now. I just knew I wanted Ivy and whatever future came with that.

The few times she'd brought up the contract, I tried to change the subject. I was so scared she'd want to walk away with the million dollars and leave me in the dust, so I chose to ignore the topic. I didn't want to hear her say that our love wasn't worth more than that to her. It would break me. More than anything I'd ever faced in my life, Ivy leaving would break me.

I heard the front door open and wondered what Ivy was taking outside until I heard a male voice. A voice I'd know anywhere.

"Richard, watch out!" Ivy yelled.

"You stole them from me," he roared. Sandro was hot on my trail as I ran down the stairs, but before I even hit the bottom step, I heard a loud crash and it felt as if my heart literally stopped.

I bolted into the living room and saw Ivy lying beside the ladder she'd been on. She wasn't moving and my dad was on his knees, looking at her with huge, frightened eyes.

"I tripped on the table," he slurred. It was like things were happening so fast, but my mind was working too slow to keep up with it. I knelt beside Ivy and moved her face so I could look at her. I placed my hand on her chest and realized it wasn't moving.

"Baby?" I asked.

She wasn't breathing.

She wasn't breathing?

Oh my God, she wasn't breathing.

"Sandro, call an ambulance!" I yelled. Ivy wasn't breathing, and, like a movie, my mind played back every conversation we'd ever had about CPR. I remembered her voice, "See how she tilted her head back? She's opening the airway."

"Open her airway," I whispered to myself. My hands were shaking uncontrollably, but I tilted her head back just enough and I held her nose shut as I pulled her mouth open. I breathed my breath into her and waited a moment before doing it again. I placed an open hand on her chest and put my other hand over it before I pushed down twenty times, then moved back to her mouth.

I don't know how long it lasted; it felt like too long, like a lifetime, but eventually someone had to pull me off her. They placed something over her face and got her onto a stretcher before I realized the paramedics were in my living room. I looked around for Sandro and found him standing against a wall. He had tears running down his face, and I imagined I did as well.

"Where is he?" I asked.

Sandro looked to the floor beside him and I moved to see my father laying down, crying. He had blood coming from his nose and I figured it was Sandro's doing.

"Make sure they take him. I'm going with Ivy."

He nodded at me, and I walked out behind the men, pushing my wife into the ambulance. I climbed in and felt numbness until I heard one of them say they got a heartbeat.

I felt hope surge through my body and cried as I watched them continue helping her breathe. I wasn't ashamed of my crying, and I didn't hold in an ounce. I'd been so scared she was dead, and I was scared she might not make it still.

"Please be okay, baby. I need you so much," I whispered. I remembered Ivy praying on the plane and for the first time in my life I uttered a prayer to a God I wasn't sure existed, asking him not to take away the only light in my life. I didn't stop praying. I couldn't.

We arrived at the hospital and they immediately took her into a room, but I wasn't allowed to follow. A doctor finally came out and pulled me into another room, asking me so many questions that I was confused.

"How did she get hurt? Did she hit her head? How long were you performing CPR before the paramedics arrived? Is your home environment safe? How far along is she in her pregnancy?"

The last one shook me out of my own crazy thoughts. "Pregnancy?" I asked.

"Yes, do you know how far along she is?" he asked again. He looked up from his clipboard and saw my shocked expression. "You weren't aware she was pregnant?"

"Absolutely not. I wouldn't have let her on a ladder if I'd known she was. There's no way she knows, either."

"Are you sure about that?"

"Positive." I had no doubt that she didn't know. If it was even true. We'd made sure she was on birth control right from the beginning of our relationship changing. "She was on the pill," I said.

"Well, birth control isn't one hundred percent effective to begin with, but has she been sick lately? Been on any antibiotics?"

"Yes!" I almost yelled. "She was sick right after Christmas and had to go to the doctor. She had antibiotics then."

"I'd say she's about three months along, then."

"But she, uh," He was a doctor, but I still felt strange sharing Ivy's private information in front of him. "She's had a couple periods since then."

He nodded. "That can happen from time to time."

"Is she going to be okay?" I asked after he jotted down his notes.

"We think so. She hit her head pretty hard, which knocked her out. When she landed, it stalled her heart as well but, you did the right thing by performing CPR. You actually saved her life, Mr. Landis."

I felt like weight continued to drop off me with every word he uttered. "When can I see her?" I asked. My voice cracked, and I knew if I didn't get myself under control, I'd break down in front of the doctor.

"You can head up there now. According to the nurse, she's stable. She isn't awake yet, but that could be our fault. We gave her something for the pain and it puts you to sleep, usually."

"So," I paused to take a deep breath before continuing, "is the baby okay?"

"We're going to bring in an ultrasound tech as soon as she's awake. There wasn't any bleeding, which is a good sign, but of course we want to check."

I walked upstairs and found the room the doctor told me she was in. She was attached to a heart monitor and had a tube that I assumed was oxygen in her nose. The beeping and the smell of the hospital caused my heart to pick up speed again. My wife almost died and now I was staring at her sleeping body. It was surreal.

I slowly walked across the room and sat on the edge of her bed. I was scared to touch her at first, so I ran my finger up and down her arm.

Hours passed before she finally began to stir. I was still sitting in the same spot, ignoring how uncomfortable I was when she opened her eyes. She tried to move but sucked in a painful breath and grabbed her head.

"Zane," her voice cracked. "What happened?"

"I'm not completely sure how, but I guess my dad ran into the ladder you were on," I answered barely above a whisper.

"Your dad." She thought about it for a moment before she looked at me with huge eyes. "I tried to warn him because I was afraid he'd fall through the glass table, but he tripped and hit the ladder. I don't remember anything else though."

"The fall knocked you unconscious. You stopped breathing."

"I did?" she asked.

"Yeah, I had to do CPR."

Her eyes grew even wider. "You did?"

"Yeah and do you remember me telling you if you ever made me do CPR on you, I would do it and then kill you myself?"

"I remember." Despite her pain, she gave me a small smile that was so beautiful I almost forgot what I was saying.

"Well, my killing you is going to have to wait awhile."

"Why is that?"

"Because according to your blood work, you're pregnant." She didn't respond.

Her face lost its color and then she turned beat red. She froze in shock and I almost laughed but couldn't since I didn't know how things were going to go once they did an ultrasound.

"I fell really far," she said.

"The doctor said you didn't bleed, which is a good sign, but they're bringing in an ultrasound machine as soon as we let them know you're awake."

"Okay." She nodded then shook her head. "I'm really pregnant?"

"Apparently." I smiled.

"But I was on birth control."

"I guess when you got sick a few months ago, the antibiotic canceled it out."

"Oh, my gosh!" she whisper yelled. "I knew that! How could I have been so thoughtless about this?"

She looked like she was about to cry, so I leaned forward and gently placed my hands on her face. I let the tears build in my eyes, not caring about them. "You scared me so bad, Ivy. I thought I lost you. You weren't breathing, and I felt like I was suffocating without your beautiful eyes on me. I love you so much that it hurts sometimes and I want to ask you to stay with me. Stay with me forever."

"Because of the baby?" she asked. "I didn't do this on purpose, Zane, I promise."

"I don't think you did, but I want you to stay because I love you and can't imagine living without you." I answered. "The baby is a bonus to keeping you," I chuckled.

The smile she gave me told me her answer, and I gave her a chaste kiss before pulling away so I didn't hurt her. "I'll go get the nurse," I said before standing up. She grabbed my hand, and I looked down into her eyes that were filled with tears.

"I want you to know I've been hoping you would ask me to stay for quite some time now."

"I was scared you wouldn't want to stay. That you'd take the money over me."

"The money!" she said, dropping my hand and looking away, lost in thought. It felt as if she'd dumped a bucket of ice water on me as I watched her think about the money. She turned and looked at me and grinned.

"Just kidding."

"Ivy," I took a deep breath through my nose and blew it

out. "If you weren't in a hospital bed and pregnant right now, I'd, well, I don't know what I would do. But you drive me crazy."

She wiggled her eyebrows at me.

"You are such a brat," I said before heading to the front desk to get the nurse.

* * *

WE WERE SITTING in the room, watching the tech getting the machine set up, and I, personally, was sweating.

Ivy wrapped her fingers around mine and I pulled her hand up to my lips and held it there. The lady finally rolled up Ivy's gown and placed the wand on her stomach. She moved it around quite a bit and began taking measurements.

"Would you like to hear the baby's heartbeat?" she asked, and we both nodded. She turned on the volume and we heard the beating of a heart. We listened and Ivy laughed and cried, causing the wand to slip away.

"Sorry," she laughed again. The woman smiled at her and placed it back on her stomach to finish gathering the information she needed.

"So, I'd put you about fifteen weeks into your pregnancy." The ultrasound tech said. "That means you're already in your second trimester and if you're lucky and the baby cooperates, we can probably find out the sex today, if that's what you guys want."

"Wow, yes! Definitely." Ivy looked up at me. "How crazy is this? Fifteen weeks and I didn't even know I was pregnant at all. I don't even feel different."

"There are rare occasions where women don't know they're pregnant," the tech said.

"My mom's biological mother didn't know until she was almost at the end of her pregnancy. I always thought that was so crazy, but now I guess I can't think that anymore."

"Okay, it looks like we have a baby that isn't too shy," the woman laughed. "Are you guys ready?"

"Yes," I answered. I felt a strange feeling bubbling up inside my chest.

"It's a," she paused for dramatic affect I assume, but all it did was annoy me. "Girl!"

I smiled at Ivy and leaned down to kiss her.

"Looks like your due date is going to be September twenty-first."

Ivy smiled at me, and I couldn't remember a time in my life that I felt so much happiness.

"Congratulations, Mom and Dad." The tech handed us a few pictures she'd printed off, and I stared at my daughter. I was going to be a dad, and I'd die trying to be the best I could be.

CHAPTER THIRTY

Zane

The hospital released Ivy the following morning, and we went home to a clean house. Sandro texted me the day before letting me know that my dad had been arrested again, and the police needed me to come to the precinct to give them my account of what happened.

I walked into our bedroom to tell Ivy where I was going and saw her staring at her belly in the mirror.

"Is it just me or do I literally look pregnant now?" she asked. I laughed because it was like finding out she was pregnant forced the bottom part of her belly to pop out just a bit. She placed her hand over her belly and I looked at the tattoo of my name on her finger, instead of a wedding ring.

Remembering her face as she got it kept the smile plastered on my face and I walked up behind her, so I could see my own tattoo.

I'd gotten the ivy plant starting at my heart and wrapping around my side. It was all over my back and went down one arm all the way to my wrist. Ivy covered me and when she'd seen it she almost cried since she didn't know I was getting it.

"I think you look a little pregnant now," I agreed.

"How wild is this?"

"It's incredibly wild. Did you tell your parents?"

"No, not yet. It hasn't really sunk in yet."

I hesitated before asking, "Are you happy?"

She immediately turned around and wrapped her arms around my neck. "I've never been happier or more content in my entire life."

"I'm glad you feel that way because I'm happy, too." I kissed her before pulling away. "How are you feeling?"

"I feel really sore, but it's more my muscles, which is kind of weird. I feel like I ran a marathon or something."

"The doctor said you'd feel sore for a couple weeks." I sighed. "I have to run to the police station to give them my statement since I didn't get to yesterday."

"You're pressing charges against your dad?" she asked, seeming concerned.

"Absolutely," I answered. "There's no way he's getting away with this, Ivy. He could have killed you or our baby, or both."

"I'm not saying you shouldn't press charges, but I think something else needs to happen."

"What do you mean?"

"I think you need to try to convince him to go to rehab or something."

I let out a humorless laugh. "Yeah, that'll be the day. He's had an entire lifetime of family and love pass him by while he wasted away in the bottom of a can of beer. I don't think he's ever going to get to a place where he's ready to be a man and get his issues under control."

"Zane, I know I hated your dad for everything he did to you and your family, but I'm starting to wonder if his demons are just so dark that maybe he's scared to walk away from all he's ever known. Just think about what I said, okay? We're having a baby and I want to be able to share the excitement with everyone. I don't want to worry about my kid going to visit your mom because your dad might be drunk."

Understanding registered. She was trying to correct a decades old mistake to protect our daughter's future.

"I'll talk to the police today about it and see what I can do. Maybe if he agrees to rehab, I won't press charges. I'll have to wait and see what he says, too."

"Promise me we'll try to help him. I don't think anyone has ever really tried before, and I don't want to add to that number."

I gave her a quick kiss on the forehead and headed to the car. On the ride, I thought about how lucky I was to have found someone that would want to look past the ugly baggage I came with. Someone who wanted to stay after seeing the skeletons in my closet. For so long I thought I was doomed to live a life like my father. I'd already been addicted to drugs, alcoholism wasn't a far cry.

It was always a shadow at the back of my mind, that one day I would be the spitting image of him. I was afraid to love because I didn't know if a day would come where I would be so drunk, I'd hit her.

What if life turned crazy, and I fell into the cycle I so badly wanted to stop? What if I hurt my wife? What if I hurt my daughter?

My breathing started to turn painful, and I pulled over

into a restaurant parking lot. I pulled out my cell phone and opened my pictures. I'd taken a picture of Ivy holding the ultrasound picture the day before and made it my background immediately.

I stared at Ivy and felt my heart rate start to slow. I could never, ever hurt this woman. I knew in every fiber of my being that nothing I could ever face would be enough to cause me to choose anything over her and our baby.

She deserved so much, and I'd already failed at giving her what she asked me for. She'd made me promise to give her adventure, and I felt like I hadn't given her enough of that. I didn't even give her a wedding day. All I succeeded in doing was showing her what a jerk I could be that day.

I smiled down at her picture and knew exactly what I could do to make things the way they should be. I may not completely deserve someone as amazing as her, but I was too selfish now to give her up. Especially now that we'd created something incredible.

CHAPTER THIRTY-ONE

Ivy
August

"You lied to me," I said, staring directly into my mother's eyes.

She giggled. "How did I lie, sweetheart?"

"Oh, don't you sweetheart me, you deceiver." I was lying on the couch in the basement and my mom was perched on the edge near my head. "You told me it was beautiful, and you loved every single minute of it, but pregnancy is kicking my butt."

I felt my eyes fill with tears that immediately made their way down my cheek and into my hair. "I feel like a failure as a mom already because this isn't fun. My back hurts so bad and I can't breathe when I lie down. I missed nausea the first trimester only to have it in the end. I'm thirty-seven weeks and I feel like I'm going to throw up every day. I feel like a crazy person for complaining about things when some people can't even get pregnant, but, Mom, it's not fun."

"Ivy, just because you're pregnant doesn't mean you have to enjoy it. It doesn't make you a bad mom, and it surely doesn't make you desensitized to other people's pregnancy journey. Pregnancy isn't always sunshine and rainbows for people, and you just happen to be one of those people."

"I still feel like a failure. I thought people were supposed to tell you that you glowed when you were pregnant, but all anyone keeps saying to me is that I look pale and Sandro said my feet look fat."

"Sandro told you that your feet were fat?" Her eyes widened.

"He did. He held up a football beside my foot and," I sniffled and fresh tears fell from my eyes. "There were actually similarities."

"Honey, I doubt there were many similarities between your foot and a football," she laughed.

"I'd pull off my sock to show you, but I can't reach it."

I heard someone coming downstairs and looked over to see Zane. "Hey babe," he said. He walked over and kissed me on the forehead before giving my mom a hug. "Sorry I missed you guys coming in. My dad had a family day at the halfway house today and asked me to be there."

"Don't worry about that." Mom patted him on the arm. "I'm glad your dad is doing well."

"Me, too. I was worried at first because he was in so much pain, but I think things are looking up now. He said he still gets headaches but I guess that's expected."

"Well, I'm going to go up and help everyone with decorations for the baby shower."

"I still can't believe you all drove here." I shook my head at my family. My dad had rented a bus and drove every single member of my family to Colorado. I think I would have hated being on that bus, but everyone showed up in good spirits. They were all upstairs at that very moment, decorating my house in pink for the baby shower only a couple hours away.

"I can't believe you're shocked. You're our child, Ivy." She laughed again, like I was the funniest person she knew. "I couldn't imagine us all not being together for something like this. Our first granddaughter!"

She kissed me on the forehead and headed upstairs, leaving Zane and I alone. "Have you figured out if you like the name or not?" I asked. I'd come up with the first name and asked Zane to choose the middle name, but he was having trouble finding something that felt right to him.

"I'm pretty confident today. I've said her whole name over and over in my head and I think it's perfect," he answered.

"Good!" I smiled. "Let's go upstairs so we can announce it to everyone."

He grabbed my hands and pulled me up beside him, but instead of heading for the stairs, he wrapped his arms around me. "I love you," he whispered.

"I love you, too, Zane. So much."

When we walked into the living room, my eyes almost fell out of my face. Everything was pink. There were streamers and balloons, table cloths on the couple of tables we'd borrowed for the food and gifts. There was even a pink throw blanket on the couch.

"Where did that come from?" I asked, pointing to the blanket.

"I made that." Grandma Murphy walked over and hugged me. She'd done it each time I walked into a room today, and it made me smile every single time. "You're such a beautiful girl, Ivy."

"Thanks, Mama."

"Okay, I think everything is set up, so we're going to start cooking and then we'll get started. Trina and her family should be here in about an hour, so it'll be perfect timing." Pop said when he walked out of the kitchen. Ever since he'd received her number after he found the contract, he and Gram had basically adopted her into the family. I wouldn't be surprised if our own daughter called her Aunt Trina.

I went and sat beside Aunt Sam on the couch in the living room. "What happened to your hair?" I asked.

"I don't even know if I can talk about it yet without screaming," she answered, and I heard my mom and Uncle Ryan start laughing.

Sam usually had very, very pink hair. It was her signature look, and I couldn't recall her hair ever being any other shade than what she started getting at the age of sixteen. But something had gone incredibly wrong, apparently, because her hair was very, very purple. She looked like a plum.

"New hair stylist?" I asked, trying hard to cover my humor.

She narrowed her eyes at me, having caught my near laugh, and said, "I think if I ever go back, it'll be so I can egg the place."

"She probably smarted off about something and the lady got her back by ruining her hair!" Pop yelled from the hallway.

"Oh, shut up, old man!" she yelled back. Pop showed up in the doorway and shook his head.

"Now, see? That is exactly the kind of behavior that should have gotten you fired the minute I met you." He grinned at her before walking away, leaving my mom and I laughing at her facial expression.

She leaned close to me and whispered, "Had he fired me, he would've had to hire three more people. I'm the best mechanic he's ever had."

"I heard that!" My dad said from behind us. "Lest you forget, I was also a mechanic there once."

"Yeah, I was counting you in that statement," Sam said with a straight face. She wasn't expecting the confetti Dad sprinkled on her head, but she was out of her seat, chasing him around the house before anyone could blink an eye.

"I swear," Mom laughed as she sat beside me. "If I wasn't certain that Sam wasn't adopted, I'd make them get blood work done just to see if they were really brother and sister."

"They do act like it, huh?" I smiled when I heard my dad yelling for someone to get out of the way before I heard the back door open and slam shut.

"They've been like that since the second they met."

TRINA ARRIVED, and we all piled into the house to eat before we started the shower. I was getting really excited to see everything we'd received for the baby, and I was almost as excited to announce her name to everyone.

Once we were all in the living room, Zane and I stood in front of the room and he yelled for everyone to quiet down so he could make an announcement. It took a few minutes, but our families gathered around us and quieted enough for him to talk.

"So, we've been working on a name for quite some time,"

"No, you've been working on it. I've had the first name

picked out for what feels like forever," I interrupted and everyone laughed.

"Okay, okay. Anyway, Ivy picked the first name, and I picked the middle, so I'd like to introduce," he held his hand toward my belly like he was presenting something, "Kayne Azalea Landis!"

Everyone cheered, and Graham cringed like he already hated the name. I didn't mind, though. He was wearing four different shades of black, so his taste obviously couldn't be trusted.

"One more thing," Zane yelled over the voices. "He looked down at me and smiled before getting down on one knee in front of me. I was confused until he started speaking. "Ivy, being the idiot I was, I didn't allow you to have a beautiful wedding like you deserved. I rushed you off to a church in Las Vegas and a few weeks later handed you a simple wedding band. You didn't get to put on a beautiful white dress or walk down the aisle toward me on your father's arm." He paused to look over at my dad. "Sorry about that Brennan." He looked back at me and pulled a simple but beautiful diamond ring out of his pocket. "I'd like to ask you to marry me again. Marry me the right way this time, with all our family and friends there to witness it. Marry me again because of how much I love you."

"Zane," I said after a few seconds of silence, "you haven't exactly asked me anything."

He laughed and I smiled at him. "Ivy, will you please marry me again?"

"Of course I will. I'll marry you a hundred times if that's what you want."

He stood and hugged me before moving to add my

diamond ring to the finger that already had my wedding band. They were exact matches.

"We'll get you a better band, too, if that's what you want," he said.

"No way! This was the first ring you ever gave me. It's mine," I said and stood on my tiptoes to kiss him.

"You might as well get married in every state just to make sure it's official. You'll already have two states under your belt after this one." Sandro said. He was leaning up against the wall and everyone thought he was hysterical. I just rolled my eyes before sitting down in my chair.

"Enough about getting married for the second time, I want to open presents now," I said, rubbing my hands together over my huge stomach.

I was tearing into the first gift Zane handed me before his hands had even let go of the box.

CHAPTER THIRTY-TWO

Zane
September

When Trina called and told me about a possible job, I didn't tell anyone. I felt so guilty about not telling Ivy right away, but I felt conflicted and wanted to make sure I knew what I was doing before I sat her down.

Trina seemed to call me every couple days, and even if Kayne wasn't keeping Ivy and I up all night, I still would have been annoyed. All I wanted was to enjoy my daughter's first few days without my agent hounding me about deciding.

Alina Dent was a director, and apparently she wanted me for a script that had recently landed in her lap. All I knew was that I'd be playing a supporting role, which was more than I could have ever hoped for.

There was something missing though; joy.

I'd waited years for this to happen to me, and yet here I was staring at my ceiling, wondering why I wasn't happy about it.

I kept trying to picture my life as an actor with Ivy and Kayne in it, and it didn't work. That wasn't the only problem. I tried picturing the man I was now as an actor and there was something wrong with the pieces because they just didn't fit.

I gave myself two weeks to think about my answer before I finally called Trina back. She was roaring mad that I'd taken so long, but when I told her I didn't want the job, she sounded relieved.

"You didn't want me to take it?" I asked.

"I don't know why I felt that way, and I hope if you still want to act you won't let me hold you back, but I hoped you wouldn't want this anymore."

"Why didn't you just tell me?"

"I didn't want you to think it was because I didn't have faith in you, which I absolutely do. I just want you to be happy, and I don't believe you were happy acting," she said. I absorbed her words and felt so much relief in them. She didn't think I was a failure.

"I'm glad you're around, Trina. I don't know what I would have done without you," I admitted.

"Finally!" she yelled and laughed. "I have a verbal confirmation that I haven't been a terrible agent."

I laughed with her. "I guess I haven't been very vocal about how much I appreciate you."

"I won't lie, for the first year of our business relationship, I thought you were a punk that hated my guts."

"Oh, I definitely hated you. Until you saved my life."

We were quiet for a moment, remembering the shape I'd been in as a teenager.

"I'm gonna get off here, T. I have to go tell Ivy the news."

"You haven't talked to her about any of this?"

"I didn't want to tell her until I knew for sure, just in case something changed my mind."

"Good luck, Zane. Even if I'm not your agent anymore, I still consider you part of my family. I'll see you soon," she promised and hung up before I could mess up her confession with my smart mouth.

I smiled before laying my cell on my desk and making my way upstairs.

Ivy was sitting in the middle of the bed, feeding Kayne. She looked up, and a grin stretched across her face.

"Hey, Baby," I said. I walked across the room and sat beside her.

"Where have you been?" she asked quietly. I looked down and watched Kayne. She was struggling between sleep and hunger, eyes closed, only sucking on the bottle every few seconds.

"I was talking to Trina. I've got some news." I glanced up when she didn't reply and noticed her face had turned white.

"What's the news?"

"Don't say anything until I'm done talking, okay?" I asked, and she nodded. "Okay, well, a director wanted me for a role, but I turned it down."

"But-,"

"No," I cut her off and smiled. "Please let me finish telling you what I have to say before you tell me what you think."

She sighed and grumbled, "Fine."

I chuckled before continuing. "Trina called a few weeks ago to tell me about the possibility of the job, but I've been struggling with trying to figure out if acting was something I still wanted. I couldn't picture myself in that kind of life anymore, so I decided it wasn't something I needed to do. It's not just about you and Kayne, although you're both part of the reason. I made the choice completely based on what I wanted and needed."

We stared at each other for a minute before she raised her eyebrows at me. I rolled my eyes. "You can talk now."

"Ugh, finally! You know I hate when you do that."

"Yeah, being quiet for five minutes is pretty difficult for you."

"It really is!" She laughed and shook her head. "Anyway, do you want to know my real opinion?"

"Of course."

"It scares me a little that you're walking away from the job. What if no other jobs come your way?"

"I don't think you understand, Ivy. I'm saying I'm walking away from acting. Completely. Forever."

"Are you serious?" she asked, shocked.

"Yes!"

"I'm slightly shocked right now."

"Good shocked?"

"Good and bad, I guess. I mean, what if you end up hating yourself for doing this? I don't want this to be something that comes between us later."

I brushed my thumb across her bottom lip and leaned in to kiss her.

"I will never regret this decision. Honestly, you might since I won't be making more than a typical salary once I get a job."

"Oh, shut up! You know I could care less about that." Ivy got serious and asked, "What do you think you will do?"

"Cop?"

"No!" she rolled her eyes. "I grew up with a cop, our kid is not going through that."

I laughed and shrugged. "I don't know what I'll do right

now. It's not something I need to know for a few months, anyway." I sighed before telling her the worst part of it. "We should probably move, too."

Elation filled her eyes. "Really?"

"Yes? Why does that make you happy?"

"Zane, I absolutely hate that window in the living room! It freaks me out every single night when I have to walk by it from the kitchen."

"There are curtains ..."

"Don't care. Hate the window. Best news ever."

"Alright ... well, that went better than I thought."

"What will we do about Sandro and Rayna? Zariah starting school worked out perfectly for her, but the other two need jobs still."

"We'll probably keep Rayna on once or twice a week, but I'll recommend Sandro and her for other jobs. I know a few people that might hire them."

"Do I get to fire him?" she asked, joy coming back into her expression.

"You can fire him, but that won't be official. He can't have that on his record."

"Yeah, yeah! I know that. Man, I can't wait!"

"Let's at least wait until we move into a new house. Give me a few months to iron out a few details for their future, if that's what they want."

I laughed when her shoulders deflated. She was hopeless.

THE FOLLOWING MORNING, I was sitting in my office again, going through emails when Trina's name popped up. I figured she'd changed her mind and was going to encourage me to stay with acting, but I was surprised to see that Tommy, my old acquaintance, had been arrested.

I had no idea how Trina got her information, but she was usually in the loop about most things that involved my past.

Seeing his name in the article made me more confident in my decision. I wasn't sure how strong I would be around the same situations that got me in trouble to begin with. I blamed no one but myself, but I didn't want to put myself in a bad situation I might not overcome.

I felt bad for Tommy. He didn't have an advocate, and I wondered if Trina would be able to find someone to mentor him. If he was going to be in jail for a while, maybe that was the perfect place to start helping him.

It really seemed to be working with my dad, to which I was thankful.

He had to miss the birth of his first grandchild, and that was hard for him. He said he cried all day, knowing he wouldn't be able to meet Kayne until he was out and at home.

"Hey, brother," Sandro said as he walked into the room and sat down across from me.

"What's up?" I asked. It used to drive me crazy how much Ivy seemed to like Alessandro, but the more I saw her interact with her brothers, the more I realized that was exactly what he was to her. Now he just annoyed me because he always seemed to be around.

Ivy liked to remind me that it was my doing, so it was only fair that his presence drove me crazy as punishment.

All in all, Sandro was a member of the family to the both of us now. He was Uncle Sandy, as Ivy liked to call him, and I was grateful we had him.

"I was actually going to talk to you about taking the night off tonight." He smiled a crooked smile. "I might have a date."

"You might have a date? How does that work?" I laughed.

"It's a 'maybe' because I have no idea if I can get off work. I work for a jerk."

"I think I've been a pretty good boss lately!"

He smiled again.

"Yeah, take the night off. You deserve it."

"Thanks." He stood to leave and stopped in front of the door. "Whatever you do, don't tell Ivy or she'll want to dress me and do my hair or something."

"You don't have hair," I reminded him.

"Knowing her, she'd figure something out. A wig?"

"I hear she's great with dealing with toupees."

"So you see why you can't say anything?" he asked.

I stood and walked out the door and into the basement before looking back at Sandro.

"Sorry, dude. I just think it would be way too funny," I said before I ran up the stairs.

The sound of him running after me followed me until I reached my room.

EPILOGUE

Zane

Kayne's birth was something that altered my life. I knew I was going to be a dad while Ivy was pregnant, but my universe shifted once I held her in my arms for the very first time. Her hair was blonde like mine and we weren't sure she'd have gray eyes like Ivy until she was about a year old. When I look back at the pictures, we took at our second wedding, I can't help but notice all the similarities there are between our daughter and us. She'd only been a few months old at the time, but anyone could tell Kayne belonged to me and Ivy.

Something none of us really saw coming was Kayne's immediate connection to my dad. He didn't get to hold her until she was nearing two months old since he'd been in rehab, but the second she was placed in his hands, it was like this cord attached her to him and nothing could sever it.

She became his little cheerleader, even before she knew that she was. Although there were times when he struggled, he was eventually able to get to a place where he felt like he was fighting for himself. That was something his sponsor stressed from the very beginning-that getting clean for anyone other than yourself was setting yourself up for failure. But he found the strength to do it, and he did. I'd never witnessed my parents so happy, and I refused to let any of us get back to a place where they couldn't be.

I didn't think their unhappiness was a possibility, though, because Ivy and I sold our house and moved three doors down from them. When Kayne turned five, Ivy decided she wanted to have another baby, and it only took me a few months to be completely on board. I was so scared that I couldn't love another child the way I loved Kayne, but, again, when I held my son, he tilted my world with his tiny hands.

Roman's black hair and green eyes surprised us. He didn't look like anyone in our family. Brennan decided Roman looked like someone from his family. They had no record of what his parents looked like, so it was very possible that Rome took after his biological grandparents that none of us had ever met. Then again, there was the joke everyone seemed to enjoy about him being the mailman's kid. Ivy hated it more and more every time she heard it.

WITH MY PARENTS living three doors down and Sandro living right beside us, a comfortable life in Colorado became a dream come true. Ivy helped free me from something I didn't even know I needed freedom from.

I'd held on to acting for so long that I thought it was what I needed. I thought if I could just get my life back to where it had been before my addiction and downfall, then I would be able to prove to the world that they had no idea what I was capable of, but when I heard Ivy singing to the kids at night, I felt on top of the world. I had no reason to prove anything to anyone outside of the four walls of my home anymore.

I still couldn't believe how much joy she took in firing Sandro. She giggled the entire time and actually jumped up and down like a little girl on Christmas Morning. He threw her in the kiddie pool when she finished firing him. He claimed she got way too much joy out of doing something so horrible. Little did he know, I'd written his recommendation for another family that had been inquiring about him, so he had a great opportunity ahead of him.

* * *

WHEN WE CELEBRATED our five-year anniversary, we decided to do something special. Since the fifth year would have been the end of our marriage if we hadn't fallen in love, Ivy said she wanted to renew our wedding vows. She wanted to add another state to the list of states we'd been married in. Sandro got a kick out of that. So, Ivy, Kayne and I flew to Niagara Falls, and I promised my wife, for the third time in front of an ordained minister, that I loved her and wanted forever with her. I told her the third time was enough because it was ridiculous how much I'd spent on marrying her every time. She just giggled and walked away.

I tried telling her no once our tenth anniversary came around; I promise I tried, but I couldn't. We ended up in Florida that time, on the beach. She wore a cute little yellow dress, and Kayne and Roman were both able to be a part of that one.

* * *

WHEN I WAS GROWING UP, all I ever saw in my future was darkness I never thought I'd be free from. Even after I was free from addiction, I was too scared to open my eyes to see anything good in my life. Then this girl showed up. She was pretty annoying, and she was wielding a wrench half the size of her, but somehow her light started to invade my line of vision. It surrounded me until it was the only thing I could see. I don't know where my life would be if I hadn't met Ivy in that little hole-in-the-wall-town in Ohio. I don't know what kind of man I would have become if there wasn't a constant laughing sound in my home, on a daily basis.

I can truly say I don't know what I would have done if I hadn't fallen in love with the greatest thing that ever happened to me.

I pulled her into the darkness with me, but she clawed her way out for the both of us.

REDEMPTION EVER AFTER

Years and Years Later

. . .

IVY

"I don't know about this, Babe," Zane said from the front porch. I closed my eyes and tried to breathe slowly through my nose. He'd said the same thing four times already.

"Zane," I slowly responded. "Stop."

He grumbled under his breath. It was strange how even as he moved closer and closer to forty years old, he still did things like grumbling and growling. Sometimes the growling was sexy, but at this moment, it was annoying the crap out of me.

Kayne honked the horn of the SUV and waved, a giant grin splitting her face. I smiled and waved back, trying to tell her how proud I was with just my eyes.

She'll be fine. I reassured myself.

It was the very first time she'd be out on the roads alone, without either Zane or me keeping an extra eye on the things going on outside the vehicle. She pulled backwards, then drove away towards a little more freedom than Zane wanted her to have.

I heard a crash come from inside the house and flinched.

Roman was going to be the death of me. If not me, then every single thing made of glass that we owned.

"I'll go see what happened," Zane said from behind me. "It looks like Rosa's outside and I know you two can't go five minutes without talking."

I would have given him lip, but what he said was entirely true. Ever since Rosa had moved to Colorado, my life was even more fulfilled than it had been before. I knew I missed my family with all my heart, but my life here with Zane was perfect. Rosa and the incredible things she brought to my life were added bonuses I didn't know I needed. And four of those bonuses were trailing her around the small garden beside their home.

Four kids! Rosa and Sandro had gotten married eight years prior, and they already had four children. The twins, Enzo and Isaac, were five years old. Giovanni was three and Luca was one. Roman, my eleven-year-old monster, seemed to always get into things he shouldn't, so I couldn't imagine life with four of him.

I chuckled under my breath as I made my way towards Rosa. She seemed to be a better mom than me when it came to order. Her boys were always so well behaved; even the baby. My kids liked chaos, but that was okay with me. Zane and I were kind of chaotic people, so they fit perfectly into our life-puzzle.

"Hey, Rose," I said a few yards away so I wouldn't scare her. She was down on her hands and knees pulling up weeds I wouldn't have even noticed had it been my garden. I suppose that's why I didn't have a garden. Or plants.

Her head popped up, and she grinned like we hadn't seen each other in weeks. "Hey!" Rosa stood and dusted her hands off on her work jeans before straightening the yellow bandana on her head. "Was that Kayne that just left?" After giving me a hug, she went back to sorting the plants.

I sighed, but the smile remained. "It was. She played Monopoly with Zane and wagered a drive on her own if she won. Obviously she won."

Rosa laughed. "What would she have had to do if she lost?"

"Clean the pool by herself." I couldn't help but laugh with her. I was the one that convinced Zane we needed a pool, and I didn't even do that job alone. It was awful. I glanced down at Rosa and noticed she was chewing on her lip so hard I wondered if she'd started bleeding. So I asked, "Are you okay?"

She huffed and sat back on her feet. "Sandro is going to kill me, but I can't keep it to myself. You're literally my best friend, so it's impossible not to tell you. He's crazy for thinking I could keep a secret like this!"

"What's going on?" Fear hit me hard. Fear that she'd tell me she was going to be moving far away from me.

Rosa looked up into my eyes and smiled. "I'm pregnant."

My jaw dropped open. Pregnant. My little sister was pregnant. Again. "Was this baby planned?" I asked quietly.

"Absolutely! I told Sandro a week ago, and he was so excited he gave himself a high five. Then he ran around the house with the boys for over an hour with the Nerf guns." She shook her head and then continued. "He's forty-four."

"Is that a problem?" I asked as I sat on the ground beside her.

"Of course not, but I can't help but think about the fact that by the time this baby is twenty, he'll be in his sixties. I would be a liar if I said I didn't think about these things, you know? I knew what I was signing up for when I married a man fourteen years older than me, but I didn't think he'd really want to keep having kids. I honestly thought he'd want to stop after the twins."

"Do you want more kids?"

She grinned, turned red, and laughed. "I want as many as I can have. Even if that makes me sound like the craziest person on earth, I don't care. I completely understand why Mom and Dad had seven kids!" She glanced down at her dirt-covered hands and asked, "Have you ever regretted not having more kids?"

"Sometimes I wonder what would have happened if we'd tried one more time for a baby, but I also feel like nothing, or rather no one, is missing from our family. I felt content and complete when Roman was born."

She nodded. "Sometimes I wonder if I'll one day regret not becoming a lawyer. I haven't felt regret since the moment I decided, but there's always a chance. Once all my kids are in school, maybe I can pursue it if it's something I want. But, who knows? How you feel about not having more children is exactly how I feel about staying at home with the kids. I feel content and complete, even if I want to keep adding more kids."

"Well, I'm not complaining. I love having nephews to spoil! Although another niece would be fun to have close to me, too." Zane's sister had a daughter, but I would have loved to see Rosa with a little girl as well.

"Sandro is all about us only having boys, so he doesn't have to learn anything new. I honestly don't mind having another boy."

"Do you ever think it upsets Mom and Dad that the rest of us didn't have over one or two kids? I mean, Graham's thirty, and he's still not even married. You're his twin," I laughed. "Do you think he'll ever get married?"

"I think Mom wishes there were more grandkids near them, but I don't think they really have opinions about how many babies we should each have." Rosa grinned over at me before checking on the boys that were now playing with the dirt. "With Graham, you're about as informed as I am. I know many people say that twins have this crazy bond, and while I do feel a connection to him I don't feel toward the rest of you, I would say I'm closest to you because I live close to you. That's not to say I wouldn't be as close to you if I still lived in Ohio, but you know what I mean." Enzo walked over to us and picked up the small shovel she'd laid aside. "Be careful," she said to him before coming back to the conversation we were having. "I think Graham will eventually find love, but who are we to say he hasn't already found it in just being single? I mean, didn't it take Jake close to ten years to get up the nerve to actually ask Zariah to marry him? They had the weirdest, long term, long-distance relationship I've ever heard of."

"Don't even get me started!" I practically yelled. Thinking about my brother and his relationship with our former cleaning lady's granddaughter was enough to give me hives. "How anyone can date for ten years while living in two different states is beyond me!"

"Me, too. But that's my point. We decided on the family life. That doesn't mean all our siblings will. Parker and Sawyer are just now looking into adopting a child, and he's almost forty."

"I could barely stand to Face-time them in the first few years of their marriage. I mean, how many times a day do you have to kiss your spouse? And do you have to do that in front of other people?"

She laughed. "Apparently, they did."

"I wish I'd been there when Mom yelled at them," I said, giving Rosa a knowing grin. We'd all heard about the conversation, but no one would say exactly what she'd said. So, we were all left guessing how it went.

A flash of black caught my eye, and I looked up to see Kayne pulling back onto our road. By now, Zane's mom was standing on her front porch waving as she passed and pulled into the driveway. I smiled, feeling especially thankful that we lived in this small subdivision. There were five houses here, meaning only two families lived here that we weren't related to. I had a horrible wish that they'd both someday move and I could buy the houses for my kids, or maybe even Rosa's. I'd never tell Zane that I wanted to live in a little colony just made up of blood relatives. We watched shows like that from time to time, and he griped about the kids needing to be around other bloodlines because they were going to end up marrying each other. I usually rolled my eyes and left him to his silly rantings.

"I better get back," I said, pointing over my shoulder. "Zane will probably badger the girl to death with questions about driving safety."

Rosa laughed but said, "He's a wonderful dad. She's lucky to have him."

I smiled, thinking back to before I'd even known I was pregnant and how Zane saved not only my life, but our daughter's life as well. "Yeah. We all are."

* * *

Months later, Rosa gave birth to another baby boy. They named him Marco Daniele Romano. The fun part about the new baby was that there were two new arrivals all within a month. Shortly after Rosa shared the news with me, Emma, Zane's sister, found out she was expecting her second child. Lucy was born less than two weeks after Marco.

"Do you think they'll have more?" Zane asked one night when we were in bed.

"Emma?" I questioned.

"No, she said she thinks she's done. Lucy has colic, and it's really hard since Betty is tearing everything up." He shook his head. "I still can't believe she named her kids Betty and Lucy."

I smiled at him in the dimly lit room. He was still so handsome, and I sometimes still felt flutters of butterflies when he looked at me like I was his entire world. "She's an actress," I said, referencing his sister. He cringed. He still had trouble accepting her career choice, even if it had been nearly a decade. "she can literally name her babies whatever she wants and the world will love it. As for Rosa, I have no idea. She wants another one, I think, but with five kids under six years old, who knows what will happen?"

"What about you?" he asked, and my heart stopped.

"What about me?"

"Do you ever want another baby?"

My eyes grew wide, and I had the smallest of panic attacks. "Uh…" I had no words.

Zane started laughing, and he laughed hard. I wrestled with feeling complete relief and wanting to kick him off his side of the bed. "That wasn't funny," I said, my voice a little shaky. Don't get me wrong. My kids were the best thing that ever happened to me in my life. They were the beauty I was most proud of in my world, but pregnancy was not kind to me. With Kayne, I'd swelled so much, but with Roman, I was constantly sick. There were endless days of having to stay in bed or lying on the couch while Zane took care of Kayne. Medication couldn't even keep much of the foods I ate down, and when I went to have him, I ended up needing a c-section. It was by far one of the scariest days of my life. It was then that I decided I wasn't sure that I could go through the uncertainty again.

"Oh, man," he chuckled, wiping his eyes and then reaching for me. "That was so funny."

"You're a jerk." I smiled, glad when my heart rate went back down to normal.

He pulled me close to him, wrapping me tightly in his arms. "I love you so much, Ivy."

My eyes stung, thinking about how lucky I was. "I love you more."

"Impossible," he whispered, right before his lips covered mine.

Made in the USA
Monee, IL
01 March 2021

61640280R00154